I WILL DO ANYTHING FOR HER

MIRIKA MAYO CORNELIUS

Author of the best selling Curse the Cotton

I WILL DO ANYTHING FOR HER

An Akirim Press Publishing
Book Cover by Akirim Press/Mirika Mayo Cornelius
www.akirimpress.com

<u>Acknowledgements</u>

I first and always thank God for the giving of his Son, Jesus, to save me, and I acknowledge and confess that without Him, I have and am nothing.

I love you, son, forever. May you forever find comfort and strength in the Lord all of your days. Husband, love you. Parents, love you.

mirikacornelius.com

I WILL DO ANYTHING FOR HER

Casey's very first interaction with a male was a brutal one, and it was when she was the age of eleven. Now that she's a young adult, she's never given herself the chance to trust and love anyone, must less a man, due to the scars left open from her past...until Tony.

The only problem is, what she thought was trustworthy, loyal and lovable about Tony was actually an obsession that he had for her, and she'd missed all the signs until it was too late.

TABLE OF CONTENTS

I Will Do Anything For Her

I WILL DO ANYTHING FOR HER

Chapter 1

She ran. She ran until she couldn't keep her clothes from falling off her, tripping up on the way back to her home that seemed so far up the road. Panic and pain disturbed the entire foundation of her life as she screamed out loud, tears drenching her face as she continued looking back, staring back at the empty road. She wanted to wake up. She thought it was a bad dream, a nightmare, but it wasn't. She wanted her mom.

"Mama," she moaned through her aching chest as she ran up the porch, trembling as she dropped her keys against the door. She looked back down the road again, pulling her torn shirt back onto her shoulder and finally opening the door. Her pink backpack fell to the floor as soon as the door came open, and she rushed to put the locks on. Right beside the front door were two high back chairs. She moved them in front of the door and then ran back into the bathroom. She'd become sick, and her stomach was in knots while her privates weren't so private anymore. She was in agony.

As the toilet filled with her morning breakfast, she saw the blood for the first time dripping from her panties that she let fall to the floor.

"No, no," she cried as her freshly cleaned school uniform had already turned a whole other shade from the grass and mud that she was dragged across and pushed into before she was punched in her side. Shoving all of her clothing off of her small, frail body, she fell into the tub, looking back at the part of the attack that she had finally escaped from - her clothes that clung to the bathroom floor.

Another smell ravaged her senses, and it was that scent that terrified her. It ate through her youthful skin like a viral, incurable rash, and even after she turned on the hot water and lathered the soap in her hands, she still smelled him after violently scrubbing.

"I can't get him off," she moaned hopelessly as the scent wouldn't leave. She took the soap suds and began scrubbing out her nostrils until she could taste the soap in the back of her throat. "It won't come out!" she cried terribly as she pulled herself to her knees underneath the beating shower and just cried, becoming more and more afraid of what to do the longer she knelt there.

An hour went by and the water had grown cold thirty minutes ago. Finally, she reached up from her fetal position and turned the shower off. She wanted to be numb, but the cold water wasn't cold enough as it only made her shiver in agony.

The house was quiet, and as she stepped out of the tub, the only sound that paid her company was the water dripping from her curly hair to the floor. Each time it hit the tile, she jumped, afraid that something she couldn't see was there with her. She kept looking around until her attention went to the bathroom door.

He was inside the house. She felt with every fiber of her being that he was going to be standing in the hallway, waiting to attack her one more time while no one was looking, while no one heard her screams, and while everyone was at work. He knew everyone was at work just like he knew she had missed the bus and was walking to school. It was her first time ever missing it since she started middle school. Her and her friends would meet at the bus stop, but today, after her mom went to work, she forgot her lunch. As she started to walk out of the house, she turned back to get her food. On her way back out, the brown paper bag tore, and all the food fell to the floor.

As she rushed to get another bag, she heard the bus. It was going to be the sweetest sound that she'd heard that morning because that was her only rescue from the curse that followed when the bus took off down the road, leaving her standing on the front porch with a repacked full sack of lunch, ready for school.

The idea of opening the bathroom door emptied buckets of despair inside her soul. She began to sob uncontrollably. "Leave me alone! Leave me!" Then, she started to scream and continued screaming, staring at her destroyed school uniform on the floor, refusing to pick it up.

Suddenly, she stopped screaming, reached inside the linen closet, pulled out every towel on the shelf and began wrapping them around her legs, buttocks, stomach and chest. With trembling fingers, she turned the knob on the bathroom door. It opened, and she fell backwards in fear, her arms flailing intensely as she squeezed her eyes shut and waited to be harmed again but nothing happened. No one touched her.

She stood up, shutting her screams down to strong pants of hesitant relief. Walking forward, she leaned into the doorway and peered out into the hall. Everything was as it was when she came into the house. Even the chairs were at the door, unmoved.

With the towels still consoling her body from the slightest touch of the still air, she went into her bedroom, shut the door, moved her nightstand in front of it just to be sure she would hear if someone came inside, and she went to sleep, shuddering under the bed sheets, the only touch that was familiar and safe. By the time her mother got back home, she had already cleaned up, behaving as if it was just another normal day after school except it was the most abnormal day ever, one that would change the way she viewed everything and everyone around her.

Chapter 2

Years Later…

"I'm going."

"You stop. Now you just stop right there."

"No! Get your hands off of me, Ma!" she shoved her mother back like she was a stranger. "You know I don't like to be touched, so why would you put your hands on me if I don't want you to?"

"What has happened to you, baby?" her mother asked hopelessly, not offended by the shove that she took from her daughter. "I'm tired of seeing you like this. One day you just stopped talkin' to me, hugging me…just like what you claim now…that you don't like to be touched? Since when? We were always close and…"

"Mama," she stared emptily into her mother's eyes. "People just grow up, and this is how I grew up. You're a good mom. Always have been. I'll do anything for you," she said as she turned to exit the front door, "Just don't touch me."

"I think we need to see a …"

"Stop thinking," she said as she slammed the door behind her.

"Casey! Casey," she called, but she knew it would have done no good. Casey had changed overnight seven years ago, and she never went back to the original happy little girl she once knew.

~.~

"I knew I would find you out here. I thought I told you to meet me back at the house, and just like always, you think my house is…"

"Here."

"At the lake."

"What's wrong with you coming to the lake?"

"Girl, we live on the same damn street. *That's* what's wrong with it?"

"We don't live on the same street."

"The same block then. Scoot over."

Casey just sat there, ignoring her friend's request, so Dia just shoved her way onto the jagged boulder beside her, joining her at the water's edge.

"Are the rest of them gonna be there tonight?" Casey asked.

"Of course!" she replied excitedly, raking her fingers through her hair. "This is gonna be the best park party that ever hit this side, better than the last ones."

"Do you think so?"

"I know so," another voice answered, catching Casey by surprise. He was one of the guys, the main guy, who wanted her all to himself, except he didn't know how to make that happen anymore.

Casey looked back, and when she laid eyes on him, she dropped them to the ground again without a care for entertaining him. He noticed the way she seemed uninterested, but his desire to pursue her grew even stronger. Therefore, he made his way behind her as Dia got up from the boulder, full of giggles, and motioned him to sit down while she walked off to take a smoke.

As he slid next to her, she didn't look up nor did she make any gestures to let him know that she even wanted him around.

"So you're gonna act like you don't want me here?"

"How's that?" she asked, finally looking up and into the lake.

"You won't look at me. You never look at me anymore, but you also never tell me to leave."

"I don't own this rock. You can be here if you want to be here, with or without me sitting here."

"Talk to me then. You can't just let me sit with you, look at you, you know, and check you out and stay quiet on me when I try and get to know you again." He leaned over and picked up a rock to toss it into the lake, trying to disturb her concentration. "You gotta at least tell me what's wrong."

14

"Nothing."

"Casey…"

"I'm just quiet."

"May I touch you… right here?"

She immediately turned around to see where he was going for, and she hesitantly said, "Yes." Her hand laid flat against the boulder, and it was there she finally felt the gentleness and warmth of his hand penetrate and soothe her tense nerves. He slowly moved her hand from the boulder and spread his fingers so that hers fell into his grasp.

"That wasn't too hard, was it?"

"No. I never said it would be," she lied, "but you also never asked before. Is there any reason why you need to hold me?"

"Yeah." He glanced back at her friend, gave her a nod toward the trail to let her know that was where he was going to be with Casey, and then, he stood up. "Come on."

"You wanna let me go now?"

"No, no I don't, but I will if you want me to. I really want you to walk with me. Will you do that?"

With no more hesitation, she stood up slowly from the boulder and walked with him. There was no more conversation until they were a good distance from Casey's best friend Dia.

"I finally noticed something about you. It's all about what you don't say," he smiled. "Like if back there you would've told me to let you go, you would have meant just that, and I would have let your hand go, but you didn't say that. You asked me if I

15

wanted to let you go now, and I don't." He stopped walking and stood in front of her. "I don't ever wanna let you go, Casey, but you have to tell me what's wrong. You're the sexiest female around here," he whispered, "but you're mean as hell…at least that's how you come off to me. I remember you though. You changed after we were about to make lo…"

"What's there to remember?" she asked, slowing her breathing as a form of relaxation so that memories wouldn't resurface of a horrible time she constantly distanced herself from each day..

"You used to like me, just as much as I like you. You were on time and, now you barely make it. You walk strong, but before you walked brave. You used to see me, but now you don't want to. I didn't turn that bad looking overnight, did I?" He moved his hand toward her cheek, but before he was able to touch it, she stopped him with her eyes. When his eyes finally met hers, he continued, "And before, your eyes were bright when you would see me, but now, they …"

"I'm fine."

"I hear you, Casey. You have to tell somebody, and you can tell me."

"Are we done walking?"

"Nah," he said, glancing back at Dia who was giving him every signal to keep going. "Nah, we're not done." He moved from in front of her, and they continued their stroll. It was quiet. He no longer said anything. Instead, he allowed his touch to say it all, and by the time they'd reached the bridge at the other end of the lake, Casey finally spoke.

"I remember, too. I remember when I wasn't like this, when everything wasn't this hard." Tears fell from her eyes as

16

she thought about the way she pushed her mom away for years because it was the only way to keep silent, to keep her mother happy. She also realized how she'd pushed Tony away for a while, all because she was afraid, afraid of everything, good at hiding her fear behind an unbothered façade.

While she was surrounded by only Tony's presence, she noticed how his touch made her feel. She hadn't felt a decent touch from anyone in a long time, ever since someone indecently touched her. It was such a relief to not have to fight off a hand. His fingers around hers felt like all the protection she needed in that moment to release all that she had hidden inside. She didn't understand why she felt she had to release it, but she did, and she wanted to do it with Tony, the only man whom she'd ever given a little of her trust.

"Come here, Casey," he beckoned her into his arms as she fought back a fit of mourning that he knew was too much for just a hand embrace. She needed to be held, and he knew it. "I'm right here. I won't tell anyone. You don't even have to tell me, but I'm still right here." As she slowly allowed his arms to embrace her pain, he spoke once more before standing with her in silence. "I will do anything for you. I'll do anything to see you smile again, Casey. I miss that. I miss you. You don't miss that?"

As her tears soaked his shirt, she responded in a low whisper, not an answer to his question, but the answer that loomed over her since she woke up. "It's today." She squeezed his shirt as the memories of the attack that happened years ago bombarded her body as if it was happening at that very moment.

"Casey, come on," he called, easily removing her from his body in order to try and read between the tears at what had been destroying her in silence. "Casey, you can't even hide it anymore. Whatever it is, it's making you turn into somebody else. What's hurtin' you, babe? Who? What's going on? Is it your mom…is something going on at the house? If so, I got you. Say the word." After a moment of listening to her cry, he finally spoke something that had been on his mind a while. He had already figured what it could have been, but he never wanted to face that it could have happened to her. "Did somebody rape you, Casey?"

Her breathing stopped, however, the tears never slowed, and then she answered physically, afraid to say the word *yes* out loud as if speaking it would bring it back again. She started to pull away from him, but Tony wouldn't let her go. Suddenly, she appeared terrified, and before she screamed, he voluntarily let her loose. That was all the answer he needed. Her actions told him yes, she had been raped, and he wanted to make her feel like she was safe again.

"I'm Tony. It wasn't me. I'm not that man, Casey," he pleaded with her. "You know me. Look, look, look…" he said, reaching on the side of his belt, pulling out his pistol, and laying it on the ground. "I got nothing to force you to do anything with me, and you know I never tried. You know that."

She stood there, her hardcore demeanor displaying one that was distraught, a side that she'd hidden from everyone, only showing her true fears when she was under her bed sheets each night feeling the same protection that she felt the day she was raped years ago – covered up all over and alone. She was safe.

She glanced at the gun on the ground. "It's not your gun that scares me. Nobody was there to help me. Everybody was doing something, so nobody missed me. Nobody waited on me," she continued in her tears. "Nobody made sure about me, that I was okay, and nobody came back for me."

"You wanna talk more about what happened?"

"Today happened! Today!" she screamed.

"Hey, hey, now, Casey," he stumbled, unaware of what or how to handle the situation at hand, so he fell on his knees and held out his arms to her. "Come on now, don't even think about it. Come over here, and I'm right here. I'm right here now, and it won't happen again. Today is a new day. It's your new day. I promise. I promise you that, baby, so come on."

She walked over to him and voluntarily went down into his arms, burying her head into his chest, and as she did, her friend was spotted running toward them, but with a lift of his hand, Tony stopped her. The palm of his hand let her know that she should stop and give them space. He watched as she placed her blade back into her pocket and walked away slowly. Then, he kissed the top of Casey's head until she was able to gather herself. They continued strolling until he was able to get her mind back to a place where she could at least become reserved once again, then he departed, leaving her with Dia but promising to be back for the park party.

Chapter 3

"So," Dia sang, understanding that Casey didn't know that she'd seen her broken down in Tony's arms, so she faked it. "Did you and Tony get close, closer than before? You know you two look good together, always have. So…is he coming?"

"Yeah, he is. And we never were far apart. I just had some stuff on my mind for a long time, and he finally figured me out."

"Oh yeah?"

"Yeah," Casey smiled, "he did."

"So what…y'all had some sort of long talk because your ass doesn't smile, and you just did," she laughed. "Pearly whites and a lot of tongue," she continued, believing they made out behind the trees.

Casey nodded, her smile never leaving her face as they strolled far past the boulder and to the corner of the eerily quiet neighborhood.

"When we were little, there were children on every street, and now look at this place. It's barren with just us and a couple of children who probably wish school was already started just so they can have some friends to play with on the regular."

"This is our neighborhood. No kids belong here."

"What did you say?"

"You heard me. This just isn't a place for kids, not with people like us in it."

"I don't know what you think is wrong with us, but…"

"Everything…because we don't know how to leave." She turned back to Dia. "We just don't know how to leave."

"Leave?"

"Yeah, like the rest of the people our age. Leave." She walked away. "See you at the party tonight."

Dia just stood there, pondering what she said, until finally shouting, "I just don't wanna leave! Why go when I love it here? This is where we are from."

"Exactly," Casey continued walking, whispering her reply under her breath as she noticed she was happier than what she'd been in a long time. As she walked back home, staring at the flowers in between the cracks of the sidewalk, she heard footsteps moving through the grass at a rapid speed. The sound was faint, but it sounded like running.

Immediately, the sound reminded her of her own past, on the same exact street. She looked up, rapidly breathing, believing she was hearing things because she saw no one. Turning around to see if Dia was still there, she saw nothing but emptiness on the street and the same sound of fear, feeling of fear.

She reached in her pocket and pulled out her blade. No one was supposed to be home at that time of day. She spun around in circles, just about to call Dia, but then she saw him. He was walking, pulling on the front of his pants and tightening his belt.

Suddenly, she felt ashamed, and instead of feeling like the strong, untouchable female she was earlier that morning, she felt small and weak, simple and raped. Since the day she was raped, she avoided him. When she was still in school, she would take the long route alone, never catching the school bus on her street but two blocks down. She did everything to avoid him. Although she was legally an adult although a teenager, she felt like a confused child. He wasn't supposed to be there. He wasn't supposed to be home.

She knew something was wrong. He'd already left that morning. She saw him leave. She'd always seen him leave, and she would never step from her house until he was gone. It was always early, and she set her alarm clock to it each morning. Watching him get inside his car was like watching a scary movie, but the horror never had an ending. It was only during certain parts of the day that she felt safe to be outside alone, and on that day of all days of the year, he was outside, and she was all alone…again.

He saw her. Their eyes locked, and Casey shook inwardly while her body ached outwardly. She didn't know if it really hurt because just before she saw him, she felt fine. Now, she felt a bitter cold, totally opposite of the smile Tony pulled from her deepest wounds. It wasn't over. It wasn't ever going to be over. He was raping her all over again without a finger and without a word.

She choked. As the sweat poured from her palm while she gripped the blade at her side, she tried to scream at him. With every ounce of her being, she tried to shout and rebuke him with her rage, the rage that continued to rehearse never ending circles until it became depressed at the redundancy of having no escape nor ending. The shout never came.

He licked his lips, grabbed a bottle of beer from his driveway, put it to his mouth and drank as he cut his eyes at her as she walked by. She smelled him all over again although he was more than twenty feet away. The same scent that was caught inside her nose for many years made her stomach turn to knots. As she passed by, turning from him and toward her home which was only a short distance away, he called out.

"Hey…"

That was all she heard before taking off down the street, the same way she did when she was a little girl. Everything felt the same way, except for this time, she had the right key in her hand to open the door. When she got inside, instead of barricading the door, she turned on the alarm, and there she waited with the knife aimed directly at the door, trembling, waiting on him to bust through so she could finally kill him.

Chapter 4

"Pop them bottles!" Dia shouted, as Casey came around the corner. The park was all set up how it usually was when they had a party of that size. They would invite the neighbors to food and music, and there were already buckets of food for the elderly in the neighborhood. Everyone was checked on and accounted for...everyone. That was how they kept everyone off their backs and the cops at bay.

The merry-go-round was full of food, wrapped up in aluminum pans and cases of beer and bottles of alcohol stacked behind a pile of sodas, so there was enough for everyone. The party was set to last all night long, beyond the food running out. At that point, there would be endless drinks located inside a locked up SUV that was parked and ready. It was supposed to be a party to remember.

"What's up, Dia!" Casey said as she approached her. She spoke to all the others, about five of them, unloading and getting the music started. The speakers already blasted, and people were straggling in behind her early, already taking the plates from the merry-go-round to head back home.

By the time the sun had gone completely down, the party was live, and everyone was having fun, socializing and most of all, taking a load off. It was so dark until hardly no one was recognizable, but everyone was having a good time. Even Casey's mom stopped by the park to get something to eat before it got too late.

"I see you're feeling better than earlier. That's good," she said, wrapping up her to-go food tighter and looking around at everyone. "You all really feasted it up this year, didn't you? How much of your money did you put in on this one, Casey?"

"It looks like you and everyone else appreciates it, too," Casey smirked, but it was barely a smile. Her mother approved of any smile she could get. "And no worries, Ma, whatever money I put in just fed you."

"Well, I'm gonna get back to the house and eat it. Your crowd is a bit different from what I'm used to. Get home when you can…safe."

"Nothing's going down tonight, Ma. It's just a party, just like the other times. Just a party." She leaned over and kissed her mom on the cheek, something that rarely happened, startling her.

"Well, thank you for that one. I wonder what brought that on." She leaned in and kissed her back. "I love you, Casey." She looked uneasily over at her daughter's crowd of friends, nodded at them as they held up bottles of alcohol and tipped them to her, and then she walked to her car and drove away. As Casey watched her mother exit the street safely, someone walked up behind her, placing his hands around her waist.

"Come on over here with me, baby." It was Tony. She knew he was there before he even spoke and put his hands around her waist because of his scent. He always smelled good. "Let's talk."

"Hey, Dia," she called as Tony guided her body in front of his to the other side of a huge oak tree that sat slightly on the outskirts of the park. "Dia!" she called louder until Dia finally heard her. "I'll be right back."

"Why she gotta know everywhere you go? You with me," he said confidently, knowing that only ten bullets with nine machetes would keep him from protecting her.

"You know why."

"Yeah, I guess I do," he sighed. "Y'all are like Bonnie and Clyde. You know she told me when to come out there to see you earlier today."

"She did?" she laughed. "Figures"

"Yeah, that's because she knows what's good for you. Who…who is good for you."

"That's you?"

"Who else?"

When they reached the tree, he pulled her in close and moved her hair from her face before kissing her on the cheek. "You feel better than earlier today?"

"Yeah, I'm good." She glanced away as she spoke, and he knew that she wasn't telling the complete truth.

"I know…"

"Tony, I don't wanna go on like this anymore," she said, thinking about her encounter with her rapist from earlier that day. "I uhh…I'm thinking about leaving. Leaving here might be good for me."

"What's that supposed to mean?" he asked, disappointed and even hurt by her rationale. "You're my lady so how? Casey, later for that. You know I ain't goin' nowhere, and …"

"It's not about you. We've been living like this for a while now, and this way of life, I mean, we can't even call the cops when something…"

"Wait…wait. Cops? What's this about? Is it what I think it's about?" He waited. "Casey, look at me, baby," he continued, softening his voice. "It's about him? He's still breathin' around here?" he asked, inquiring about the man who raped her.

"Tony, I just feel like…"

"Is he?"

His eyes were like stone, and his entire demeanor changed only slightly but she could tell. She could always tell. Whenever he would change like that, he wasn't playing around. All she knew, all she felt, was that he loved her. He loved her very much, and he always had.

"Yeah, yeah…he's around here. I just don't wanna talk about it," she said as tears began to stream down her face, and her body visibly grew even more tense the longer she had to discuss it. He saw the anxiety and decided to change the mood.

"You don't have to cry no more," he confirmed, wiping the tears from her face. "Let's celebrate," he smiled, tickling her stomach. She got caught up in his silliness and started to smile again.

"What are we celebrating besides the party?"

"Celebratin' the fact that we're about to get tore up, that's what. Fuck this stress, baby. We're about to be laid out, and I want you to have a good time. We're gonna make this one all about you. This is about to be your party." he laughed, and they rushed back to the center of the park, ready to bury her troubles and have fun doing it.

Chapter 5

"Hell yeah, she can take another one. Whatever I do, she can do," he said, looking her way with adoration. "She can just do it better." Then, he took his shot, and just as he took his shot, she stumbled into her next one, as he leaned over and caught her as she landing in his arms. The entire crowd shouted her name over and over again as Tony laughed in his own inebriated state, however, not as drunk as Casey.

They both ended up lying down face up to the night sky as someone lightly pushed the merry-go-round so that they went round about.

"Casey, baby," he called as he reached over to grab her hand while she kept running out of breath trying to sing a song. "Who did that to you, baby?"

"What?" she laughed. "Look at that sky…"

He put his foot on the ground and slowed the merry-go-round to a stop as Casey pointed but failed to connect the stars with her finger. Then, he stood up, waved his hand to the people who were nearby to make them walk away, stood in front of her dangling feet and repeated the question but with more detail.

"Who raped you, Casey?"

She started crying as soon as he asked her the question. Instead of interrupting her, he only hovered over her, not appearing as inebriated as once thought, and he waited for her answer. He knew she would answer, so he waited.

"Don't you hate him, Casey, for what he did to you?" Then, he moved in closer, holding on to the rails, leaning over to look her in the eyes. "You wanna kill him, don't you?"

"I want him dead. He hurt me, and my mama never knew and nobody could help me because he told me…he told me…"

"He who?"

"I missed the bus, Tony, that's all I... Mr. Clange said that he didn't want to have to do it again, but he would if I said something. Shh…" She quickly reached up and grabbed his hand while placing her finger against her mouth. "Tony."

"Yeah, baby," he said as he lifted his hand up to signal his friends back over. When they got there, he leaned over to one of them and said, "End the party. Send everybody home, but you and the rest of them stay, including Dia. Turn that music up. I need y'all to take somebody a plate for me. Make it up." Then, he whispered to another before they dispersed, afterward turning his attention back to Casey.

"You need to lie down, baby. Don't worry," he said, cocking his eyes to the side and lying back down on the merry-go-round with her. "Ain't nobody gonna hurt you no more. Tell me though, if you could do something to him, what would you do?"

"I would … beat him to death," she shouted as she punched at the air like she was a trained boxer, then she began kicking. "And I would stomp the blood from his body like this."

"Close your eyes and picture yourself doin' it. Don't that shit feel good? Hit him, Casey…harder."

"I'm beatin' his ass, and he won't ever do that to me again. Then, I can walk outside before he leaves for work…" she sobbed again, and as she sobbed on his shoulder, he spun the merry-go-round with his feet and waited as the music played.

"It's just me and you always, Casey. You want that like I do?"

"Yeah, I do."

"Life, baby. Nothing can separate us…on blood."

"Who's it out there?" he hollered through the door. His voice was always hoarse, and he periodically coughed up mucus from his throat to spit it in a small plastic white cup that he kept on his porch at all times. "Whatever it is, I don't want it. It's late."

"Open the door, Mr. Clange. You didn't come out to get your food from the park party, and we got plenty left. You know we take care of everybody in the neighborhood, so here. We won't leave it out here on the porch like you're some dog. Take it. Open up."

"Well, ain't nothin' else to do but open this damn door since you servin'," he responded, more upbeat but still cautious. The door flew open, but he only cracked his screen door after surveying the young men on his porch.

"How the hell you gonna get the plate? You want us to tip it sideways so all the food can fall out?" the one in front joked, cuing his boys to laugh. "Open the damn screen and take the plate."

"Put that shit down on the porch," he responded, feeling uneasy about having even opened the door so late in the first place. He knew the guys, several of them by face, even knew their parents, but that was the first time they delivered a plate of food to his house whenever they had one of their loud parties. He never went to any of them, but he'd always had someone bring him a plate, except for this particular party.

The faces of the young men at the door turned sour. "Put it on the porch?" The leader of the group looked back at everyone, and then turned back to face Mr. Clange. "Here your mutt ass is then… a plate of food for a mangy mutt…" he continued as he leaned over as if he was putting the plate on the ground, but instead, forced his arm and foot into the crack of the screen door. Mr. Clange fought back, attempting to pull it closed, but the other guys tore the screen door back and barged in, terrifying Mr. Clange who had no weapon in close vicinity.

Mr. Clange fell backwards, knocked to the floor, scrambling toward the hallway as the guys came in with the one who took the brunt of the screen against his body holding a pistol and pointing it directly at the fearful man's chest.

"That hurt like hell man. Got food, food I made for you, all over me and all on the floor." He then kicked him in his side to halt his movement backwards. "Where you goin'? Eat this shit," he ordered, sliding the food across the floor and shoving it in his face. "You comin' with us. Get him some clothes. Make it look like he was already out." Then he instructed one of the crew to remain at the house to pretend to be Mr. Clange, to make it look like he was still present at the house.

"You stay here. After an hour of movin' around in this house, turn off the lights like you are gone to sleep and meet us back at the park. Use the back door." Then, he kneeled down to Mr. Clange, who still gripped his side in agony, believing that his rib was broken as the others came back and put him on new attire. "You look like one of us now, hangin' out. Put your cap on his head," he ordered one of the fellas, "so that he looks like one of us going to the car for these nosey neighbors." He stood back up, levering his last order at Mr. Clange. "You're coming, and you're gonna walk to that ride out front, and you won't make a sound. Pick him up, surround him, and talk like normal...put him in the truck. I'm leaving out the door after you...sayin' bye to you, the new Mr. Clange," he laughed, turning to the imitator before rubbing his shoulder. "That damn screen door hurt."

Mr. Clange ended up at the park in the middle of the night against his will. The more he struggled, the more they hit him, until eventually, he just sat there and waited until they were signaled by Tony to pull him out of the SUV.

"Leave the music playing. Take him over there to the swings, and pin him to the ground...in front of Casey. Whatever she says, you do." After they dragged him off, Tony followed behind slowly, enjoying the sound of Mr. Clange's pleas for help that no one blocks from the park could hear through the music. Once he was placed in front of Casey, her head was down, like she was asleep. It was Tony that awakened her.

"I'm here to make your dreams come true, baby," he spoke into her ear, and as soon as he did, she smiled. "It's time to beat him to death. Don't you want to...beat the man to death that raped you."

"Yeah, that would be all I ever wanted," she laughed as she kissed him on his lips. "Dia!" she called, but nobody answered. "Hey, Dia, I wanna tell you something."

Tony looked up and waved Dia on over. She had no idea what was going on, so she was a bit shaken by what she saw but didn't show it. Instead, she walked over to Casey, and sat on the other swing. "What's up, girl?" she asked, not looking at Casey but at Mr. Clange who was pinned to the ground with his eyes glued on Casey. He hadn't moved them once since he knew whom he was laid out before on the dirty ground. Dia saw his tears, and then she read the silent movement of his lips which mouthed *forgive me.*

"Is that really Mr. Clange right there, googly eyes on me, again?"

"That's him," Dia responded. "Why is he here? What's going on?"

"That's who raped me, and now I get to kill him," she continued, rolling her head back in Tony's direction, "Don't I?" Then she fell to the ground. "Is that really you, Mr. Clange?" She rubbed her hand across his face, and then fisted a large pile of moist dirt in her hand that she smeared across his face and up his nose.

"Tony..." Dia whispered. "Does she know what she's doing? She's drunk, can't even stand up. Casey..." She reached for her, but Tony grabbed her arm and yanked it back, squeezing and pulling it so hard that she thought it would break.

"Don't do that shit," he scolded Dia, taking her by surprise. "Casey, what you want, baby?"

"I'm trying to stuff up his nose so he can't breathe, but it's not workin' 'cause his mouth keeps fallin' open," she laughed. "What you do that to me for?" she asked Mr. Clange who couldn't answer due to all the mud in his air passages.

"You want us to help, don't you, Casey? Come on, and sit back on this swing. Dia, sit right here." Instead of listening, Dia drew her blade, the only weapon that she'd ever needed to get her point across, but before she ripped through his skin, another guy grabbed her other hand, twisting it until the blade dropped.

"Dia, this man raped your girl. You ain't hear her?" he asked, annoyed with her getting in the way of Casey's revenge.

"Tony, she's drunk! Casey, listen to me," she begged, but it didn't help.

"Stop lookin' at me! Make him stop lookin'!" Casey screamed in a daze, not able to take her eyes off of the man who raped her.

"My pleasure, baby."

That was when the beating started, and it went on and on as the music drowned out his calls of agony.

The swing creaked as it moved through the wind, going back and forth as her feet dragged the singed grass, pulling up all the life from the roots until there was nothing but pure dirt. That's how long she'd been there watching as they beat the man bloody.

She continued to smile at the craters that covered the moon's surface the same way she smiled at the craters that were being created on the man's face. There was a rhythm to the beating, and she'd started to hum to it. As she swung, each time the bottoms of her feet hit the dirt, there was another harsh blow to the bloody body of the man who laid there motionless on the ground. Instead of raindrops covering the blades of grass, it was his blood which seemed to glow in the dark.

"Stop." The swing stopped moving, and she stared at the broken body that lay five feet in front of her. When she saw his chest move, she stated, "Again." As her feet hit the ground with the motion of the swing, the rhythmic beating continued until there was no man left…and she finally felt free.

Chapter 6

She rolled over to sit in her bed, and as soon as the light entered her eyes, a jolt of pain reached her brain and shoved her back onto her mattress. Her head pounded under the authority of an unforgiving migraine, and all she could do was roll over in pain.

"Ma!" she called. "Ma! My head… Ma!" she yelled but got no answer. She rolled off of the bed and onto the floor, and with her eyes closed, she crawled her way to the bathroom and squinted her way through the medicine cabinet for some pain meds.

The television was on in the living room, so after swallowing the pills along with some cool water from the faucet, she stumbled in there. There her mother was staring at the television in disbelief.

"Ma, why didn't you answer me? My head is…"

"Mr. Clange was beat to death at the park last night." She turned to face her daughter. "You were out there all night long. I didn't hear you when you got in here, but I know you were out there because I went to sleep later, after one-thirty, thinking you would come home at a decent hour. What happened to him out there?"

Casey remained quiet. She didn't remember him even going to the park last night because if he had been there, she knew she wouldn't have even gone. "Ma, I don't know. Beat to death?"

"Yeah, beat to death! Ain't ever been no violence like this around here since I been here, not like this."

At those words, a rage rose in Casey that spilled over. "Open your eyes, Ma! No violence? Ma, look at me, and you're cryin' over him? Him? Forget him! Whoever beat him, I can guarantee you he started it. He wasn't nothing but a shit starter, and somebody finished him off."

"Casey!"

"Don't call me, Ma! Don't you ever call me like you know me." Her attitude suddenly went cold, and she continued in a low tone, "You don't know a thing about me."

"Well, tell me about you! Tell me, baby," she pleaded, jumping up from the chair. "That could have been you, baby! Somebody out there murdered that man, and he is just houses down. Casey!" she called when she saw that Casey had already checked out of the conversation. "You act like I'm not supposed to be upset. What did he do to me…or you…that I should want something like that to happen to him, huh?"

Casey stopped on her way down the hall. She didn't turn around, but she answered, "You're right, Ma. Question still is, what *did* he do? Just because he got killed doesn't mean he's an innocent party." She left her mom in the living room and shut her room door behind her as she walked to the window and looked outside. Her eyes followed the sidewalk to Mr. Clange's house, and for the first time since he raped her, she felt safe. Then, she picked up the phone to call Dia. The other line picked up, but it was quiet.

"Hello? Hello? Dia?"

"Yeah?"

"Why didn't you answer me? I'm here calling your name, and you're just sittin' on the phone. My head is beat down. What the hell happened last night?"

"Casey, I gotta go. I..."

"Where you goin'?"

"I mean..."

"Wait...did you hear?"

There was silence on the line until Dia finally spoke up. "Did I hear what?"

"It's on the news. That man... Mr. Clange...he was murdered. Somebody must have caught him out there at the park sometime after we left and beat him to death. Ma was out there watching it on the news."

"Yeah, I know. I uhh...last night, you were pretty out of it. Do you remember how packed it was out there?"

"Yeah, but I don't remember getting home at all. Thanks for tucking me in." She looked up at her dresser. "Where did you put my house keys?" She put her head in between her knees. "I feel so bad right now. Migraine..."

"I didn't tuck you in last night."

"Well, how did I get here? I walked? If I walked, you came with me. I don't even remember where I..." she continued, starting to search for her keys on the floor and underneath the sheets.

"Casey, I walked home. You rode."

"What?"

"I gotta go."

"Dia…"

"I don't have your keys." Dia hung up the telephone causing Casey to redial. Dia picked back up.

"Dia, don't hang up on me. What the hell is going on? You're acting strange as fuck."

"I'm sorry, Casey. I tried…I didn't know. You never told me, and now it all makes sense. Mr. Clange…"

"What? Wait…" Casey began to tremble, and immediately, her stomach began to quiver to the point where the muscles in her neck tightened, causing her to run to the bathroom and vomit. The telephone fell to the bedroom floor, and Dia had already hung up by the time Casey got back to the phone. Casey didn't call her back.

"Ma, have you seen my keys?"

"No."

"Ma, I'm sor…"

"Bye, Casey. I'm done. Keep your sorry. You don't ever say anything, you don't damn do anything except what you want to do and say, so just go. I don't know where your keys are, just like apparently I don't know where you are anymore."

Casey's head lowered in shame, but quickly rose again because the wall that she'd learned to build around her in times of defense would never go tumbling down. Although, with her mother, she did want it to break to pieces, she didn't know how to go about ripping every fiber of her hardworking mother to shreds with the whole truth of what happened to her. Despite her tough shell, she loved her mother, but the further away she could keep her mother from her, the better off her mother's heart would be – at least that was her rationale. She wanted to handle the problem of her rape on her own instead of breaking her mom's heart. It was enough that she was broken than to have had her mom broken as well.

"Alright. See you when I get home."

She went to open the door, her mind in a frazzle while still thumping slightly from her migraine, and as she opened the front door, there Tony was staring back at her.

"Tony?"

"I came to check on you. I have your keys."

She quickly turned back to her mom, who had obviously heard everything, and walked outside, shutting the door behind her. "What are you doing with my keys?" she asked, taking them from his hand and glancing down at his waist. "And you're at my mom's house. Don't bring that pistol in or around here. She doesn't like 'em."

"My mistake, Casey. I didn't know."

"You did know," she said as she pushed past him to sit on the porch, staring down at Mr. Clange's house. Tony traced her line of vision to the house, and then he sat down beside her.

"You feel better?"

"No, I have a migraine," she paused, "And I don't remember anything from last night. I don't even know how I got home and in my bed."

"I brought you home, and I took you in the house."

"In my house? You walked through my house? You could have made my mom have a heart attack. The only person my mom expects to be there is Dia. Where was Dia? She told me…"

"Told you what?" he said looking away. "What did *Dia* tell you?"

"Is there a problem?" she asked, noticing how he changed, his posture and his voice, like he was annoyed.

"Nah, baby. Nah, ain't no problem."

"What happened last night? The news said that Mr. Clange was beat to death at the park." When Tony didn't answer, she continued. "We were the ones out there all night."

He turned back and looked her directly in her eyes. "You wanted him dead, so we killed him."

"What?" she uttered, leaning away from him totally confused, unaware of how to grasp what he just said and why.

"You heard what the fuck I said. You can't take that shit back."

"Tony, I didn't kill anybody."

"You told me more than three times you wanted that man dead for rapin' you."

"I never told you who…nobody knows who, and … and I only told you about the rape the other day when…"

41

"No," he laughed, "you told me when we were on the merry-go-round. Your ass was angry, too. So we went and brought him to you, and we did what you said do – beat him until you told us to stop, and believe me, by the time you told us to stop, his ass stopped," he grinned before going serious. "Wasn't no life left in homey when we got finished with him."

Casey stood up and nearly fell over the weakened porch rail. "I didn't order any murder."

"Like hell you didn't. Look, Casey," he said, standing to his feet, reaching for her as she backed away. "What are you backing away from me for? I'm not the one that raped you. I helped you out."

"You got me drunk." It all started to make sense as she thought back to right before she blacked out, their conversation.

"I got you your heart's desire, baby. That's what's wrong with life now." He stood directly in front of her, gazing lovingly into her eyes. "People don't know how to end it, end anything that's in the way of happiness. I told you that I would keep you safe. Anything you want."

"I didn't kill anybody."

He pulled out his phone and called Dia. "Dia." He put her on speaker. "Tell her what happened. Did she order that killing?"

"Casey," she stumbled before crying from the guilt that she'd been burdened with all night because she didn't have the strength to stop her best friend from doing something like that while not in her right mind. "I tried … yeah. You ordered it, and I watched."

He ended the call. "Why would I lie to you? I've never lied to you."

"Fuck you, Tony. Tricking me is the same thing, just worse." She shoved him aside and marched away from her house as he sat back down on the porch to smoke a cigarette, watching her make her way down beyond the home of the deceased. Each time the ashes dropped from the end of his cigarette, he got angrier at the thought of her not appreciating what he did for her. Finally, he rose from the steps and knocked on Casey's front door. Immediately, Casey's mother opened it and stared at him. She'd never formally met him before, only seen him.

"Ms. Parker, I'm Tony, Casey's friend."

She stood there at the door confused. "You already know she isn't here, so I'm not understanding."

"May I come in? I need to talk to you about Casey. I know from some past conversations me and Casey have had that your relationship with her is strained. I think I can help with that."

"You think so."

"Yes, ma'am, I…"

"That wasn't a question, and I don't like guns."

"I can't leave it out here, ma'am, but I promise I will lay it down on the floor at the door and won't touch it until I'm outside of your door. I'll just lean in and pick it up from the barrel."

"How long have you been knowing Casey? I know your face, just not you."

"For a long time now, since I was a kid."

"Come on inside, and drop the gun. Where did Casey go?"

"Down the road. Probably headed to Dia's house."

"You know Dia, too?"

"Yeah, yes ma'am. May I sit down?"

"Sure." She turned off the television and sat down across from him, on the other side of the coffee table. "Casey hasn't been right for a long time now. She doesn't like me touching her, and she never opens up to me. Once my sweet child, she no longer is. Instead, I have her, someone I don't even know." She cut her eyes up at him. "Do you know why?"

"Yeah. Something happened to her when she was young." He pulled out his pack of cigarettes. "I know you don't like pistols, but do you mind if I light up?"

She did mind, however, because of the information that he was about to reveal, she allowed him to smoke. "No. No, I don't mind."

"Thank you," he responded after lighting his cigarette and throwing his lighter on the coffee table.

"Excuse you," she retorted, offended by how he tossed his lighter onto her furniture.

"I'm sorry. Habit…but yeah…Casey was raped," he stated nonchalantly.

"Raped?" Casey's mother gasped in disbelief. "Raped? When…who? Casey?"

"She didn't tell you, but she told me because she could trust me much more. You weren't there for her when it happened, after she missed the bus," he explained, taking a deep breath.

"She couldn't trust me, her own mother?"

"No, she couldn't, and when she told me about that, she's been telling me her secrets ever since." He took a long puff from his cigarette and then put it out on the bottom of his shoe. "The only person she let's really, really touch her is me because it was me who was and still is there for her, that day and now. She tells me that you wasn't ever there, and I think that got her so fucked up to how she is today. You raped her of your presence, and he raped her body."

Casey's mother didn't actually know how to respond to what he stated because to her, it sounded ludicrous. She began to get uncomfortable, and as he sat there staring her in her eyes like there was more, she refused to show any weakness and didn't kick him out because she needed to know more. Therefore, she responded, "I never raped her of anything. Now you tell me - who raped her?"

"Mr. Clange."

"Mr. Clange?" she repeated in shock, trying to put together pieces of Casey's life that fit into what he was saying, but she simply didn't know how or when a rape could have happened and her not know about it. She finally blurted out, "He's dead. You know that right?"

"Yeah," he sang. "He is dead," he continued standing up and walking behind her to the kitchen, lifting his cigarette up to let her know he was walking it to the trash, "And guess who killed him," he said as he walked back over slowly.

"Who?"

He leaned over into her ear and whispered, "Casey."

She stood up immediately. "Get out of my house! Get out!"

45

"See that's why she can't trust you. You overact. If she would have told you who raped her, then you would have plastered her name all over the news and told every cop on the streets. She would have been known as the victim and not the vicious, and who wants that?" He walked around her as she continued to scold him, and he finally stopped again, directly in front of her. "You damn near jumping on me for telling you."

"A lie!"

"The truth."

"I'm calling the police."

"No the fuck you're not."

"Excuse me? You're in here lying on my daughter. There's a dead man that you tell me a young girl – my daughter - beat to death in a park. You and the rest of those *gangsters* were there," she stated, flailing her arms in aggravation and anger, "but as far as my daughter, she didn't kill anyone! Get out."

As she headed for the telephone, Tony grabbed her from behind, put her in a choke hold and squeezed tightly. "Nobody, not even you, will hurt Casey. Why would you want to call the cops when that situation is already done? You prove my point. She doesn't need a relationship with you or anyone else…except me. All she needs is me." Struggling to hold her still, he took her to the floor so nothing in the home would be disturbed, and after she took her last breath, he let her head hit the floor hard in order to make it appear like she took a bad fall.

From there, he removed his cigarette from the trashcan, took his lighter from the coffee table and retrieved his pistol from the floor before locking the front door behind him while waving, "Bye, Ms. Parker. Thanks for the talk."

Chapter 7

"Dia. Dia. Open the door." The knocking didn't stop until Dia unlocked the door and let her inside. When she entered, Dia stood there, her eyes filled with pain, looking at the wall away from Casey.

"What the fuck happened last night?"

Her mother was seated on the chair watching television, the captions on. She was deaf but could read lips.

"Let's go in the back room."

"Hi, Casey," her mother smiled. "Good to see you."

"Hi…I just need to talk to Dia for a minute in the back."

"Go ahead," she responded.

Before making her way down the hallway, Casey started in again. "What happened last night, Dia?" she demanded.

"I already told you!" Dia shouted. "I already said it! He wouldn't let me stop you. He twisted my arm. They all had me, and you started pushing mud up that man's nose, and Tony asked you, he asked you what you wanted to do. You wanted to kill him. They stood me there until it was over, and it didn't help anything when I yelled and tried to get away. You were laughing," she said in disbelief, "And maybe you should have because didn't he rape you? You never told me until last night."

Casey slid down the wall. "What did he look like?"

"He didn't look like much of anyone or anything when they finished. I heard it. You heard it. You kept laughing." She looked down at Casey as she stared at the wall. "You enjoyed it. I threw up. It was the worst beating I'd ever seen. I would've preferred they shot him, but they beat him. He was like mush..."

"That's enough."

"You didn't actually hit him, but you ordered it, and Tony ordered them to listen to you. They didn't stop until you told them to stop."

"I don't remember any of it, Dia." Tears began to fall from her face, not because of Mr. Clange's death, but because someone else took her control from her again. She felt lost. "I don't remem..." she choked until she cried out from desperation and agony over her own life. "Why?! I trusted him! Why would he ... he may as well have raped me, too, Dia. Why didn't you ..."

"I didn't know your getting drunk was his plot, Casey. I just didn't know. I never thought he would flip like that on you, on us. Tony just wasn't the same last night to me or you. He wasn't the same."

Casey stood up from the floor in a trance like state. She remembered when she told him about the rape, and her heart began to beat rapidly, causing her to hyperventilate. Dia reached over to grab her as she held her chest. Her eyes grew bloodshot, and she tearfully held on to Dia as she understood exactly what happened with Tony.

"I should have never told him anything earlier that day. I confided in him."

"When he came to the lake?"

"Yeah. I opened my heart to him. I felt like I could, Dia, and now he's out here taking it all the wrong way, acting like he knows what's best for me."

Dia became afraid. "Did you tell Tony you were coming over here?"

"No, I just left."

"He really doesn't want me talking to you, us talking to you."

"Doesn't want me to talk to you?"

"Yeah, that's what he told us. Man, Casey, I was scared. I've never been held against my will like that. He didn't hurt me, but in a way, he did. No, I'm not hurt, but I knew, I just knew, I would be next. Honestly, Casey, when he ended the call, I was relieved because I wasn't supposed to say anything about last night. No one is supposed to talk so we all won't go to prison or get our mouths shut for talking. You can't say anything, Casey, not now. He's looking out for us...in a way. We were all there. We participated." She paused. "When it was all over, the beating, he told me that he did it for you, so you could live again." She turned away. "I can't argue with that. I can just argue with the way it was done. Casey, they beat Mr. Clange until you said stop, and I watched Tony smile the whole way through the beating. He was smiling at you and at Mr. Clange. Me, I felt like I was in the damn twilight zone! I'm telling you, it's not like before. We, me and you, we don't have control over ourselves anymore. Not anymore. Tony is flippin' out on us."

As she spoke, there was a knock at the door. She panicked, "Casey, I know that's him!"

"He needs to stop following me, dammit," she complained as she bolted to the door, but Dia grabbed her and shoved her back.

"No. No. Just be quiet. He'll leave. I told you, he's not the same." After pretending like they weren't at home for a minute and no more knocks came to the door, she continued. "I think he's a bit more than in love with you, Casey. I think he's obsessed."

"No, Dia."

"Yes. After last night, you know how he is always saying he will do anything for you, he'll do anything to keep you safe and happy, and all you have to do is say the word?"

Casey nodded.

"Well that mother fucker ain't lyin'. Most men say the shit, but this one is real, and that's not normal. I mean, I get it. Mr. Clange raped you, so damn him, but they killed him … *twice*. I couldn't tell his body from the mud. And Tony's smile when he did it, sucking it all in like…and how he was caressing you through it. It was like you had strings, and he was your puppet master. Mr. Clange…"

"I don't care if Clange is dead, Dia. Tony shouldn't have done that to me, that's all. What he did to me was just as bad, but in a different way because *I didn't* have a say so. I was drunk."

"Who's next then, Casey?"

"Next?"

"Yeah, next. Me? When you fuck around and make me angry and he doesn't like what I say to you, what will he do to me?"

"He doesn't know what we talk about. You're reaching. He would never hurt you. From what you're telling me, if he wanted to hurt you, he would have done it last night. An argument is different than rape, so don't worry."

"I know it is, but he doesn't see that! I'm telling you, Casey. He ain't right on you. He will do anything for you, and that crap ain't all the way right. I'm telling you, Casey. I know he's a gangster, but it's beyond that. He's lost it, and I think he's lost it for you."

"I'm leaving." She walked away conflicted and annoyed with everything, feeling used and dumped. "What he did wasn't right, but it wasn't right when it comes to *me*. Fuck Mr. Clange, but now I'm involved in a murder that I had nothing to do with," she said looking back, "I'm being convicted over and over again, Dia!" she said, waving bye to Dia's mother who sat there trying to read her lips, but not able to because Casey cocked her head away from her sight, "And it's all because of him."

"Casey, be careful. My hands are tied. We roll over on him and them, he rolls over on us."

Instead of answering, Casey opened the door and left. She wasn't five steps into the yard before she noticed movement to her right. Before turning around, she remembered how fearful Dia was, and it caused her not to turn around. She knew Dia was watching, and she didn't want to put any pressure on her to come outside to her aide if anything happened. She knew it was Tony, and he wasn't trying to hide. Suddenly, she felt like all her independence was gone, and she didn't like the feeling. With every step she took, she didn't feel like Tony was trying to reach out and embrace her like he would have normally. Instead, there was an intimidation that embraced her as he remained his distance, but she ignored it as her anger swelled. She heard him behind her as if he had her on lock and chain, and before she knew it, she'd already turned to face him, lashing out in order to protect her own interests and best friend from whatever threats he made. "What the fuck did you do to Dia? She won't say shit to me!" she lied. "I knew that was you that knocked on her door. She's in there fuckin' cryin'."

He approached her, he looked to his left and right, and then walked right by her like she didn't even exist. Then he stopped, looked into the sky and then back down at the concrete beneath their feet. "Who the fuck you think you're talkin' to? I see your ass can walk these streets now like you're really my woman…and not that mother fucker's victim… not a fear in the world because I made that shit happen as a statement for anyone else that tries to hurt you, and this is the thanks you give me? You trying to bring me out in these streets right here?"

"No, Tony, I'm asking you what you did to Dia? All that other stuff you're talkin' has nothing to do with what I asked you."

"I don't know why that girl is cryin'. We didn't beat her ass," he smirked but completely serious.

"It looks like she thinks you would."

"That shit is deceiving, too." He paused to slowly admire Casey from head to toe. Then, he moved closer to her. "How do you know she didn't help us beat his ass? Did she tell you?"

Immediately, Casey knew the question he asked was a set up against Dia, and it caused her to lose her position as she backed away from him unconsciously, catching herself before he noticed. Even though she stopped, he did notice her hesitation which told him that Dia spoke up when she shouldn't have.

"I don't. I don't know what she did. It doesn't seem like something she would do. She said there wasn't anything to tell."

"She wouldn't even do that for you, huh?"

"No. Not even for me."

"That's fucked up. She ain't the friend I thought she was."

"She just knows me, that's all. She knows me good enough to know when I'm too drunk to think straight."

"But she didn't know you were raped. I knew that," he said as he reached for her hand to caress it, "Because you trust me. If you trust me, you should know that drunk or not, it's me that has your best interests at heart. Fuck all that other stuff. I got you home safe and all that. Didn't even wake moms up, with her paranoid ass," he said, knowing her relationship with her mother was never great.

She glanced back at Dia's house and then back at Tony, her senses high, believing that she had to give in to his banter just a little so things wouldn't get bad for Dia. Although Tony had always been a nice guy, he was one of the smartest and most dangerous, just never dangerous to her or Dia. "Thank you for getting me home, but about my mom, she can be somethin'. She's alright though. She's my mom. She would give her life for me, even if we don't get along. It's more my fault than hers," she said, defending her mother against all the horrible things that she probably said about her to him while venting.

"You think so?"

"I know so."

"Nah. You don't know much."

"You don't know shit about my mother," she said under her breath as she walked around him, in the direction of her home. Then she stopped to say something else because her pride and rage wouldn't tamper down to let Tony have his ego. "And you don't know much about me either. Yeah, Mr. Clange is dead, and good, but you're no better than him. You didn't protect me, Tony. You used me, got me drunk, because you know I woudn't have done that sober, if I did it at all because I don't fucking remember. That wasn't my kill. That shit had nothing to do with me."

"Okay," he spit. "Okay. And just like I said, your mother don't give that much a shit about you because I told her ass Mr. Clange raped you."

"What?" she asked stunned.

"You know what her ass told me. She told me to get off her porch. I told her that's why you didn't like to be up on people and was quiet all the damn time, except when you're with me. She didn't believe that either." He watched as Casey stood there starting to cry and break down so badly that she fell to her knees. Then, he walked over to her, leaned over and said, "She told me that Mr. Clange would never rape you, that all he ever did was work and sleep and try to make a good living. She told me that I was a liar and that she would never believe that story. Then she said that she was done with you, tired of all the problems and heartache you caused. Said you were nothing but pure heartache. And Casey, I just got up and left."

By the time he finished speaking, Casey was already sobbing with her hand in the palms of her hands as Tony picked her up from the sidewalk, catching a glimpse of Dia shutting her blinds. As he lifted her, she fell into his grasp, and he stood there for a while, proud of the lie he'd told, because to him, it was for her own good, their own good. He needed her in his life, and he would do and say anything to get that done without any interference. He was done with sharing Casey. Dia was right. He was obsessed.

"I told you that I was the only one who had your back. I love you, girl."

At those words, she pushed off of him. "You don't control me though. You should have never told my mother or anybody else, just like you should have never gotten me drunk to do what only *you* wanted to do, and just like you should have never tried to avenge anything for me. You run *your* crew… but you don't run me. I never asked you to. I never did. That isn't the kind of man I want, and I don't love you…anymore," she cried, wiping her eyes after her admission, something he never knew, "because I can't trust you. You're no good for me. Not for the person that I struggle everyday to become. You stunted that growth. I can't let you or anybody do that to me again." She began to walk away but turned to say one more thing to his face. "Stay away from me."

He stood in the middle of the sidewalk, watching her walk away, as if nothing had changed and nothing was even wrong until she was out of his sight.

Chapter 8

"Dia," he sang as he knocked lightly on the door. "Open the door. I know you're in there, baby girl. I need to holler at you for a minute."

The door came open, and Dia stood there, widening the door enough so that her mother could clearly see who was at the door in case something happened. She wanted her to read his lips. He knew she was deaf, but he didn't know anything about her other skill, and she'd secretly warned her mother before opening the door.

"Tony, what's up? If you think I was talking to Casey about anything, I didn't. You were right there with her on the phone, so you knew she was coming here. What did you want me to do, not let her in? That wasn't in the plan. She's my best friend."

"Why are you talkin' so much, baby?" he asked, as he turned to her mother then back to her. "I didn't ask you one thing about Casey, did I? You know, a sign of guilt is too much talkin' to questions that haven't even been asked."

Dia quieted.

"I thought you knew how that worked?"

"Only with the cops."

"I police this area, don't I?"

"Until you come here. You've never policed me, Casey, or any of the others. Why now? Why so different?"

He tilted his head down and to the side, away from her mother, as if he knew more than what Dia thought he knew about her skill of reading lips. "Because *we* killed somebody last night. This time you and Casey are in the *we*. I used to keep you and her out of my bullshit, but fuck it now." He glanced over to where he stood with Casey minutes ago before stepping inside Dia's house and shutting the door, nodding at her mother as she sat there, unsure of what was about to happen. "I don't mean shit to her no more, and that means, you shouldn't mean shit to her either. Tell your mom to go to the back."

"Why? She can't hear you," she responded defensively.

"Tell your mom to turn around, Dia, damn," he said growing increasingly frustrated at her resistance.

"No. She lives here, not you. I told you that she can't hear. She's deaf. You know that."

"Fuck it then." He viciously pinned her to the wall, his arm strangling her at the neck as she fumbled for the blade that was normally attached to her side, however, as she pulled at her pockets and belt, Tony raised it to her face. "You lookin' for this right here?" Then, he turned to Dia's mom, who ran to defend her only child, but Tony placed Dia in a headlock, dropped the knife under his foot and pulled his pistol.

"Yeah, Ma. See that, Dia. Mama, can't hear. I knew that shit. Her ass can see though. She sees I'm gonna choke your ass out." He started laughing. "I see you, Ma. Guess what else, I know she can read lips, too, so I'm gonna mouth this to her, and your ass is gonna watch what she does because this time *you* won't be able to hear me."

Making the situation into a game that he controlled, similar to what he did with Casey at the park, he used his mother's weakness against them both. He mouthed directions for Dia's mother without making a sound, pretending like he was whispering something into Dia's ear. He fell amused when he watched Dia's mother turn her back to them, trembling in fear.

"Now, Dia, with your smart ass. I bet you know what I mouthed to her now. I told her to turn around or I will blow your pretty head off this cute, tatted up neck."

"She did, so let me go."

He shook his head while he placed the pistol on the floor and Dia gasped for air. Then, he picked up the blade from underneath his foot. By then, the grip on Dia's neck was so tight until she fell unconscious. At that, Tony sat her in the chair, right behind her mother who continued to sob and stare at the wall. Then, he placed the blade in Dia's limp hand, and slit her wrist.

"Suicide, Dia? I thought you were better than that? At least go out in a fight, baby. If she can't love me, she can't love you either. I don't share anyway."

He then stood directly behind Dia's mother, repeating, "I just killed your daughter. I just killed your daughter." Each time he spoke, she shook. She knew he was directly behind her because she smelled the cigarette smoke come off of his breath. Finally, he stepped away from her calmly, walked to the floor and picked up his pistol again. From there, he checked outside by peering through the blinds, and once he saw that no one was there, he walked back over to Dia's mother, tapped her on her shoulder and watched her turn around to see her dead daughter as blood poured from her wrist.

"Sorry." He lifted his pistol directly at her as she fell atop her daughter, hysterically trying to revive her, but instead of pulling the trigger, he bludgeoned her to death with his gun. "She didn't hear me apologize anyway. Didn't hear me confess either."

Shortly after preparing and eating a sandwich, he left Dia's home. He didn't see Casey again the whole day until the sun set. He'd finally found her at the spot where he figured she would be, and he was right. She didn't go home. He figured she wouldn't have gone home after he revealed that he'd told her mother. He actually knew she didn't go home because as he sat in Dia's home, eating a sandwich as the dead bodies lay before him, at no point were there sounds of ambulances or police. That was the confirmation that he was in the clear and that Casey was nowhere near her dead mother.

~.~

"Psst," he sounded as he stepped from behind the trunk of a large tree at the lake. "I knew you would be out here." He walked toward her, and she removed herself from where she sat to alert him to the fact that she wanted nothing to do with him and wanted to be left alone. He didn't heed the body language, jogged over to her and slid his hands around her waist. She wrestled away, furious that he'd continued to harass her after she made herself clear that she wanted nothing to do with him.

"Didn't I tell you to leave me alone? Did I stutter?" she asked, retrieving her brass knuckles.

"Who you gonna hit with that, baby? Look, I'm sorry. Satisfied? I shouldn't have told your mother or anyone about what happened to you, but I handle shit," he smiled, before it faded away. "I thought that's what you loved about me. You really don't have to ask. I see a problem, and I'm there for you. I'm here for us. I fix it."

"I need to be alone, Tony."

"I didn't know you loved me," he said as if he didn't hear what she just said.

"I don't."

"You did."

"That shit is over."

"You never told me."

"I never could because of stuff like this. A deadened heart is the best kind because it doesn't feel anything, especially pain. You hurt me," she said, fighting back tears. "You were able to hurt me because I spoke! I told! You even told my mother. Just leave me alone!"

"Don't hit me with that brass, Casey. That crap will hurt," he warned her as he continued to approach her.

"Tony. Tony," she retorted. "Leave me the fuck alone. I'm not those other girls."

"I know. I would have downed any other female for raising a glove at me. Alright...I figure I can at least let you get a swing, a nice hit." He stuck his neck out in generosity. "Let it out, Casey. Hit me with all you got. I promise I won't hurt you. Take that shit I did to you out on me right now."

She dropped her brass knuckles to the ground. "Fuck you." She didn't want to give him the satisfaction that the hit would have made them even.

"Where you going, Casey?" he sighed as she stormed off. He picked up her brass knuckles and waited on her to turn around. She never did. Then, he looked down at her weapon. "I'll be seeing you, like I always do, even when you don't know."

Casey entered her home through the bathroom window. Her mother would crack it open whenever she was at home to ventilate the area, so she knew her mother was there when she walked to the back of the house. The sound of the loud television gave her presence away, also. After all that was told to her by Tony, she didn't want to see her mother at all, and she didn't want to talk about it. She wanted to be left alone.

As she climbed inside the window, she was careful not to make a sound, and as she planted herself in the tub, she removed her shoes in order to make her way to her bedroom. She undressed, and as she did, she stared into the mirror that hung from her closet door of the dimly lit room. She wondered what she was exactly. Ever since the morning of her rape, she'd never felt human. Instead, she felt alien, even parasitic, like something was attached to her that wouldn't let go, making her stand, sit, eat and even breathe differently than other human beings. She would watch how other people interacted with each other, but whenever she interacted, it was all wrong and ended up all wrong...just like the other night at the park.

Opening the closet door removed the shame she felt of herself because the mirror was no longer in sight. Feeling ashamed was one thing, but facing it was whole other demon that she hated looking at. She reached into the closet and yanked down a pajama tank and shorts before pulling the comforter from her bed along with a pillow so that she could sleep away from everyone and everything. She wanted to sleep inside her closet. It was at that point, Casey knew that she could trust no one, and she was all alone.

She'd been asleep for a while and awakened by a knock at her bedroom door to which she ignored at first, but when the knocking continued without ceasing, she wandered to the bedroom door.

"Mom, just leave me alone." When she spoke, the knocking stopped, but as she walked away from the door, the knocking started again. "Ma! Stop! Look, you … you already made yourself clear when you talked to Tony. Leave me alone! Whatever you have to say is too late," she quieted down. "It's too late anyway. It happened a long time ago, and … he's dead." She sat on the bed, and the knocking started again. "Ma!"

Suddenly, she was overtaken by an uneasy feeling, like something wasn't right. Glancing at the time on her digital clock, it read a little after midnight. She'd been asleep for a while, and the television was still on. The television was normally shut down at eleven-thirty every night because her mom was in the bed by twelve.

She stood up from the bed and immediately grabbed the phone. Panicking, she waited for her mom to speak from the other side of the door, but there continued to be just knocks. She called her mother's cell phone, but it kept ringing. She called Dia when that didn't work, but no one picked up, and the knocks at the door continued.

"Ma! Ma, is that you?" She slammed down the phone and prepared to fight as the door knob turned. Visions of possibly being raped again captured her mind as fear set in about why her mother wasn't talking and what was going on. Finally, the door slowly swung open.

"I came in the house right after you did. I didn't understand why you went in through the back window when I came through the front door. I waited on you out there."

Casey froze. It was Tony. "Ma?" she called. "Did my mom let you in?" she asked angrily as she tried to push her way past Tony, but he blocked her way.

"Yeah, she did. Remember I was just here earlier. She knows me."

"No she doesn't."

"Damn, girl," he laughed. "You won't let me get anything over on you, huh? Well, no. No, she didn't let me in."

Casey backed away from him confused. "What you mean my mom didn't let you in? Ma!" she continued calling, growing more concerned over the fact that her mom wasn't answering, not from her bedroom or the living room. That was when he lifted his hand, allowing something shiny to drop into his other hand.

Casey's eyes followed the juggling act he was doing, tossing the item from one hand to another, until she was able to finally make it out. She grabbed the lamp from her dresser, yanking it from the cord and attacked him, but he caught the lamp in mid-swing and tripped her off of her feet. She hit the floor.

"Remember I brought you your keys, baby?" he said, kneeling down so that she could get a good view of his face and the lone key he held between his blackened fingernails. "I figured I would need a copy of it one day, you know, to check up on you and the moms."

"Where's my mom? Give me my fuckin' key!" she arose from the floor and made an attempt to take it from him, however, he was too strong and quick.

"Hold on now. You didn't talk to mom when you came in?"

"Where's my mom, Tony?"

He looked down the hallway humorously and then back at her, shrugging his shoulders. "She ain't here."

That was enough for Casey to try to bulldoze her way through Tony until he finally just moved, causing her to crash into the wall of the hallway. She moved through the house terrified that something was wrong, and as she made her way through her mother's bedroom shouting to no avail, she turned to run to the living room when Tony grabbed her arm.

"Casey, listen." She tried to get away from his grasp, but he grabbed her other arm and held her tightly. "Casey! Stop playin'."

"I'm not playing! This isn't a joke. Get out of my house! Let me go," she continued to struggle to get loose, kicking and scratching until he finally let her go along with words that followed her into the living room. "She's dead, baby."

She stopped at the beginning of the hallway and turned back to face him. "What?" she asked as an insatiable pain and unwavering fear gripped her being as she fell to her knees in disbelief, needing help but not able to call, wanting help but not knowing where to turn.

He approached her, and as he walked forward, she turned to crawl into the living room, unable to breathe, hyperventilating. The way her mother smelled, looked, laughed, held her when she was small…all those thoughts took over her mind, but they all vanished when she came to reality and saw her mother's head on the floor next to the coffee table.

"Mama!" she rushed toward her, raising her head carefully from the floor to lay it on her thighs. "Mama, Mama, please! Wake up...breathe, Ma!" Casey's eyes traveled to her mother's fingers that had already turned purple at the tips, and it caused her to wail. "Tony, call the ambulance. Call them!" she begged, completely out of her mind, having not put the situation together in her head, until he answered .

"Why would I do that shit? Her ass fell, and dammit, I was at the wrong place at the wrong time. Can't let that shit get pinned on me."

Casey's soul furiously quaked at his words as she stared at her mother's beautiful face, caressing it like it was still warm with life. Finally, her eyes left her mother's face, and she spoke, "You killed my mother." She placed her mother's head on the floor and stood to face her mother's killer with tears running down her face, putting the mountain of pain she was in on full display.

"She was gonna turn your ass in for killin' that mother fucker that raped you," he lied. "You think I was gonna let her hurt you like she'd been hurtin' you, Casey? Your mom hated your ass. Told me some shit that only an enemy would say about you."

"She's not my enemy! She never was my enemy," she screamed, hitting her chest. "She's my mother. I'm my own fuckin' enemy! Me! Look at you. Look who I chose," she continued, stepping backwards to head toward the kitchen drawer. "You ain't shit," she stressed before pulling open the drawer to grab a knife.

"Fuck you gonna do with that knife, Casey?" He sat down on the sofa, put his leg up and pulled his pistol, sitting it on his leg. "Like I said, your mom had to die. She ain't fuckin' like me anyway, and how we both gonna be in prison for her lack of understanding on what and why we did it." He waved her over. "We, Casey. Us. Come on. Don't be scared of me now," he said as he leaned over to stare her directly in her eyes.

Casey stood there, unable to process anything that he said as her mother lie there dead beneath his feet. She wanted him dead more than she wanted Mr. Clange dead all her life, and it didn't matter, nothing mattered anymore, whether she went to prison or not. All she ached for was his death to avenge her mother, a mother whom she'd missed all of her life but never stopped loving, not for one second.

"Tony," she wept, "I hate you"

"I figured that shit, but your ass is mine. I've always wanted you all to myself, and now I got you. You'll learn to love me again. Come sit down because I wanna explain something to you. You can bring the knife. I won't hurt you, and you don't wanna really hurt me." He pat the cushion of the sofa in a welcoming gesture, but Casey didn't move, infuriating him to the point that he got up and charged her as she stabbed at him, but he grabbed her arm and threw her onto the kitchen counter face first, placing the knife to her throat. "We already have a mess in here, don't we? Mama fell, and you called me over here when you found her. Don't worry. While you were asleep, I called myself from your house," he continued as she wept. "I got in here just now, and we called who?" Casey didn't answer, so he pulled her hair and shouted, "Who?"

"The ambulance."

"You got it." His voice and temper diminished quickly, and he backed away, sitting the knife atop the refrigerator. "Your love ain't worth shit if it ain't for me, Casey. You don't think straight if your love ain't going one way, and that's my way." He held his arms out. "Come here, baby girl. If I tell you your mom was gonna separate us, she was. I did all this shit for you. You're always walking around closed in, what was I supposed to do?"

"Nothing!"

"That's not me. You know that. I've always said I would do anything for you. You used to tell me thank you."

"Not this," she cried. "This isn't you."

"No…it is. You close your eyes to a lot of shit. If I say it, I mean it. I've always been that way, Casey. Open your damn eyes." He grabbed her hand and pushed her chin up so that he could look into her eyes again. "Or are you lying to me because you still love me? Only love can make you that blind, baby. I'm One out here in these streets. Ain't that what my name is? Tony is my family name. One is my street name. You love Tony. I'm mother fuckin' One with your ass today for the first time. You pushed my ass to that today, talking shit, and after what I did for you? You think I'm out here avenging you so you can spit in my face? I went damn all the way on this shit *for you*."

"No, no… Tony, I love my mom. Arguing never changed that. Mr. Clange did what he did to me, but I don't wanna go to prison for that. You set me up. We could have left," she said, touching his hand, trying to connect with him again so that she could make it out alive. "That isn't love what you did to me. It hurt me, and I was angry with you, said some things that I didn't mean. How do you expect me to feel right now? Look at my mom, Tony. Let me go. Let me get my mom help. She's just lying there!" she shouted, trembling, "If you still love me, Tony, just let me help my mom. I didn't mean for you to think this was what I wanted. You killed my mom, Tony. My mom! You just made a mistake."

"I didn't do shit. Call the ambulance." He handed her the phone from off the wall, not paying attention to a word she said because he knew it was all a game. She took the phone. "Call 'em, and don't play that movie psychology shit with me."

She dialed. The phone rang only once, and when the person on the other end said *"911 what is your emergency?"*, she pretended like she was about to answer and slammed the phone against his temple. The phone was still in her hand as she leaped across the counter. He grabbed at her ankle but missed, giving her the freedom to lunge for the gun that sat on the coffee table.

When she landed, she hit hard, but she was able to get the gun in full grasp, turn and fire. He was right there behind her, and when the bullet hit, he fell directly atop her, struggling to breathe as the bullet burned through his chest. His eyes shut, and she shoved him onto the floor before standing to her feet. He was still breathing so she leaned over and spoke to him one more time.

"I guess cocky ass One left his gun on my mother fuckin' table."

She rushed back to the phone that she'd dropped during the shooting, gun in hand, and the emergency operator was still there. She'd heard everything and had already sent the cops and ambulance on the way.

"Ma'am, stay on the line. Do you still have the weapon?"

"Yes."

"I'm going to need you to put it down and go outside to safety."

"No. I'm not puttin' shit down. This ain't a mother fuckin' movie. I'll wait. If I shoot again, just know that

68

Tony…Tony Walker… One…he got back up, and I had to put him back down."

He never got back up, dying on the floor next to her mother.

Chapter 9

"I got nobody else but my friend Dia. She lives down the road, around the corner."

"Can you stay with her for a while?"

"Yeah." She picked up her phone to call Dia as the officer gave her space on the porch. Her stomach had already emptied itself on the side of the house, and she felt light-headed at the sight of her mother being zipped up in a body bag to be taken to a morgue. She didn't know what to do. She was all alone, and the only person who she could rely on was Dia and Dia's mother. She had no other family.

As she sat there waiting on Dia to pick up the phone, she got the voicemail, so she ended the call and redialed. After dialing four times and getting no answer, she called their home phone. She called a multitude of times, and it was odd that Dia didn't answer at all, no matter how late it was, especially after calling multiple times. Finally, she texted Dia's mom's phone. She couldn't hear it, but she always had it on vibrate and right up against her skin whenever Dia wasn't at home. Dia would always put it on her lap, just in case, whenever she left the house. The text went unanswered. Something wasn't right.

"Officer, no one is picking up. I need to go down to her house. I can walk."

"No, one of us will take you down. You're in no condition to walk or drive."

"Sure," she agreed, and in five minutes, she was on the way to Dia's home in a detective's car. She honestly felt that the only reason he was giving her a lift wasn't because of how she felt, but instead, to investigate and keep his eyes on her. He was doing his job, pretending to care in order to collect evidence though she knew there was nothing more to collect.

It didn't take two minutes to get to Dia's home. She thanked him for the ride and exited the vehicle. As she walked to the front door, she looked back, and his car was still there, waiting on her to enter.

She knocked on the door a couple of times. The house was quiet, and that wasn't abnormal being that it was late, in the early hours of the morning. The only abnormal thing was that the television was on in the living room. Casey's heart sunk. She began to panic as she remembered what just happened at her home and how the television was playing when it shouldn't have been at all.

"Dia!" she yelled, before climbing over the high bushes so that she would be able to see into the house through the sheer curtains. She pounded the windows, and as she pounded, she heard the door of the detective's car slam. He was jogging her way, but she didn't stop hitting the window. Before he got to her, she jumped back in front of the door and continued to bang, finally placing her hand on the door knob and turning. It opened. Casey ran into the house, but immediately fell back into the detective's arms when she saw Dia lying there with her wrist slit and her mother lying there atop her dead.

Casey fell to the floor, deliriously screaming and weeping her best friend's name, as the officer pulled his weapon and called for backup. She scrambled to reach Dia, but the officer grabbed her by her feet and pulled her out the door. Each time she fought him, he tackled her back down, understanding that she had completely lost her mind in the midst of all the death of her loved ones all at once.

"Casey, please..."

"Get off of me! He killed them. He killed them. I know he did."

"Who?"

"Tony!"

"Somebody could still be in the house, so you need to stay here while," he explained, looking up at the back up that arrived, "...while we clear the house. Stay put or I will have to cuff you, Casey. Please."

He didn't have to plead with her much longer. Casey passed out in his arms. When she woke up, she was in a hospital bed with an IV in her arm, and the same detective by her side, with a pen in his hand and a recorder. The first words from his mouth were, "Start from the beginning."

She stared back at him with tears in her eyes and streaming down her cheeks, while memories of her smiling, loyal and patient mother, silly, vibrant, and anxious Dia and Dia's mother, shown in her head like one long, beautiful movie. Then, she took a deep breath and spoke with a courage she'd never had before.

"It started when I was eleven years old. I was raped."

She told the full story, and the detective never charged her in the murder of Mr. Clange. He never even wrote that part down. He decided she'd been through enough pain. Casey, then, walked free.

THE END

Thank you for reading "I Will Do Anything For Her". If you enjoyed this story, please leave a review.

Now, keep reading into your special paperback buyer bonus book – MOST WANTED FELON.

I Will Do Anything For Her

Most Wanted

FELON

MOST WANTED FELON

From the outside looking in, China Daniels lives the life every woman dreams of - nice home, lovely daughter and a wonderful marriage. But in reality, things could not be further from the truth.

At the discovery of a secret that her loving husband has desperately tried to conceal, the truth unleashes a series of events that could not only destroy her family and livelihood, but will make China Daniels a MOST WANTED FELON!

Most Wanted Prologue

"It doesn't matter. All I'm asking is for a favor, that's all. You can't do that for me, Penelope? After all we've been through, I get nothing from you?" China stated completely soaked in the rain after she cut through yards to reach her sister's house on foot. She'd parked her car behind a store building where there was barely any light, especially in the rain, and from there, rushed to Penelope's house with her bag, car keys and a load of cash. "I have money…take care of Selah with it until I send you more." She pulled out the cash and pushed it through the screen door forcefully as Penelope would only allow the screen to open but so much. The cash fell to the floor and scattered at Penelope's feet, but she didn't even look down. Instead, she stared at China in disbelief.

"After all *we've* been through?" she repeated, stressing the all inclusiveness of her statement. "Is that what you just said? You mean after all you put *me* through, China, and now your daughter," she said lowering her tone. "And you say it doesn't matter? Don't you know what you've even done, China?" Penclope gazed at her in shock. "Now, get the hell off of my porch," Penelope grumbled fiercely as she shook the screen door of her newly purchased rundown home. "China, move! You can't be here!" she continued to scream at her half-sister in the middle of the night as China relentlessly yanked the screen door against Penelope's wishes.

"You're my sister, Penelope!" China finally gave up and slammed the screen door, resulting in Penelope quickly locking it. "You're supposed to be my blood, and you're just gonna leave me out here like this in the rain? You don't know the full story at all!"

"I don't have to know it, dammit, because I saw it!" Penelope yelled as she punched the screen door, her emotions riddled with rage and sadness all at the same time as she looked back into her sister's eyes.

A small child wearing a long T- Shirt came running from the back room and latched onto Penelope's leg, staring back at China from behind the screen door. "Mama?" She asked half asleep.

"Hey, baby girl. Yeah, it's your mama," China responded out of breath and glaring at her younger sister as she reached at the screen door hoping that her four year old daughter would reach back out to her. "Can you put your hand right here, baby? Mama can't come inside because I'm all wet…and I don't want you to catch a cold, you know?"

"I love you, mama. You can come in and dry off, and thank you for letting me stay at Aunt Penelope's house. It's fun over here," said the little girl as she grabbed for the latch of the screen door, but her aunt Penelope moved her hand away.

"Go back to bed. Your mom…"

"I stopped by to see you…before I go back to my new job," China quickly interjected with a lie. "I needed to see that you were okay and if Aunt Penelope is being good to you. Did she feed you, honey?"

"Yes ma'am, and…"

"And go to bed. Your mom," she rolled her eyes so the child wouldn't see her do it, "will be back again. She'll be back soon enough…I'm sure of it."

I Will Do Anything For Her

The child planted a kiss on the screen door, and it was met with the lips of her mom. That was good enough for her to turn around and go back to bed. China watched beyond her sister as her child turned into the bedroom.

"Leave, China. This time, don't come back. You're on your own." With that, Penelope closed the door, leaving her sister out in the pouring rain.

China stared back at the door's peephole while the rain placed more heaviness on her than what she already carried inside her soul. She slowly turned around as her hair stuck to her face while the rain camouflaged her tears. Suddenly, she snapped out of her saddened daze and realized that she was standing uncovered before neighboring homes to the side and directly in front of her. She could have been seen.

Rushing from the porch, she turned to the back of the house, feeling her way on the side due to the darkness and rain blinding her way, until she felt the crawlspace entrance. As she felt for the latch, it was being held together by a thin, knotted rope, so China kneeled down, unknotted the rope and entered the area beneath the house. She didn't care about any rodents, snakes or anything. The only thing she cared about was being as close to her daughter as possible before having to go on the run again. She'd just become the city's most wanted felon, so she put her head down and cried, with nowhere to go.

Most Wanted One

"Okay, are you ready, baby?"

"Go, Mama, go!" squealed the little girl as her mom pushed her for the first time on the swing at the park.

"Look at you go!" laughed her mom, China, as she watched her four year old be carried in the air by the plastic seat being held up by two chains and a bar. "Hold on tight, Selah. Hold on really tight. I'm about to push again," she warned as she reached out and lightly tapped her daughter's back. Selah giggled as the swing went back up into the air while her mom anxiously awaited the swing to return to where she was standing.

"Mom, I'm doing it, I'm doing it see," yelled Selah as she tried her best to turn around and see her mom without falling out of the swing.

"No, baby, hold on tight. I'm back here, and I see you really good. Keep looking straight."

"Push me higher!"

"Here we go," China sang as she pushed and ran around the swing to face Selah.

"Mama! I'm not scared anymore," Selah cheered herself on as the swing went back and forth.

"I know, baby girl. You're a big girl now, aren't you?"

"Yep…big and strong."

"If I can get my little girl to do that today…" spoke a woman that walked up beside China.

For a split second, China glanced at the young lady with a smile, pulled her brown, curly hair back away from her face and then responded as she spotted the woman's daughter attempting to climb onto the swing. "She's a cutie. How old?"

"She's three…three and a half years old. And yours?"

"Selah's four…and a handful might I add," China joked. "I'm China," she continued, reaching out with a handshake greeting.

"Oh…nice to meet you. I'm Raayna, and that's my baby girl Synthia with an S."

"That's pretty and different. Nice to meet you both. Do you live around here? We live right down the road there." China then looked at her daughter who was already staring at the little girl ready to play with her.

"Yeah, we live right up the road, in the opposite direction…at Dew Crossing."

"That's fairly close to us. Maybe we'll see each other again, huh?" China responded. "Well, Selah, it looks like you've had your fun. Let's get ready to go."

"Ma, but…"

"No buts…" she responded, turning back to Raayna. "It was nice to meet you and your daughter. She's such a lovely little girl, and look, she's sitting up on the swing ready for her first push." China lifted Selah from the swing and watched as the other little girl held on tightly while her mother gave it a nudge. The little girl didn't fall and a big smile came across her face. China smiled back at her and swiftly took her daughter in her hand as Selah waved good-bye to the little girl.

On the way to the car, China allowed Selah to run freely in the park. Her daughter had always loved to kick the pine cones no matter where they were on the ground, so she would find as many as she could and make a game of it all. China even decided she would kick some of them herself since the day was going so good, and it was during her kicks with her daughter that she heard the little girl at the swing whining something to her mother.

"Come back here, Synthia!" China heard the woman named Raayna call after her daughter.

"I wanna say bye to my sister."

China froze in mid-step as she listened to the child run toward her and her daughter. It had been only one year since she found out about her husband having a long drawn out affair behind her back, and there was nothing but distrust and sadness that had taken a front row seat to her shame when out in public, despite her husband sticking to her hand in glove except when he was at work.

Sean had been on the police force all his adult life, and whenever she'd gone out in public prior to the affair, she was proud to be married to whom she thought was a man who represented the good officers on the force. Sean did everything he was supposed to do as a man who upheld the law, and he even went above and beyond, turning a blind eye to minor offenses such as homeless people falling asleep in unauthorized areas or things that simply were, in his eyes, less criminal and more sit down, teach and help type of offenses. He truly had a heart to serve the people as a whole, not just lock them up with no discretion.

I Will Do Anything For Her

There was another side of Sean that China never knew anything about, however, and it suddenly struck her in the heart again as the child ran beyond her and touched her daughter. Her concentration was broken as the little girl's mom approached from behind.

"I'm sorry, China. She has a wild imagination," she spoke as China turned to face her with a load of paranoia draping her shoulders. A throbbing pain began to erupt behind her neck as the stress of the memories overwhelmed her while Raayna continued to talk. "She's always wanted a sister, so she...you know...makes believe." When China didn't respond quickly, she noticed the way China stared back at her like she was completely transparent, as if she could see straight through her.

In what seemed like forever but really only seconds, China snapped out of her gaze, glanced at Selah and Synthia and forced a smile. "Oh, I understand...Raayna. Children have imaginations. My daughter is an only child," she continued with a pause, glancing quickly back Raayna's way, "too."

Raayna nodded and rushed Synthia back to her. "Maybe you will see her again sometime, okay?"

"Okay, Ma!" the little girl sang as she skipped back over to her mother. As soon as the little girl grabbed her mother's hand, they promptly turned away to head back to the swings, however, China stood there staring until she saw the swing start moving again.

The radio played on medium volume as China drove through town on her way back home. As she made her way down the road, her mind slowly dismissing the paranoid incident at the park, her cell phone rang. She took her eyes off the road for only a second to see the caller, and when she looked back at the road, she slammed on brakes.

"Selah!" she shouted her daughter's name as she threw her arm across to the passenger's seat to act as a barrier between the front of the car and back. Her car came to a screeching halt, and fortunately, she ended up inches away from the car in front of her. China slammed her back against her seat, relaxed her arm on the steering wheel and shoved the gear in park as they waited at the traffic light. "Baby girl, are you okay? I almost got into a wreck."

"Yes ma'am. I'm in my seatbelt," she responded confidently. "I can't get hurt in my seatbelt."

China let out a deep breath of relief and lifted her eyes up to the roof of the car. "I know, baby, I know. Always...wear your seatbelt. Mama's sorry."

"It's okay, mom. You didn't mean it." Selah continued to hum her favorite song as she sat staring out of the window at the traffic. During Selah's simple song, China picked up the phone.

"Hello, Penelope, hello," she answered slightly irritated and shaken.

"Are you coming or what? I've been waiting for like thirty minutes, and I could have been doing other things besides waiting on you to get here with Selah."

"Why do you have to give me so much grief, Penelope? I told you that I would be there this afternoon, and it's just now going on one-thirty. You have got to get over that shit, P," China stated under her breath as to shield her language from Selah's ears.

"Get over it, huh?"

"Yes, Penelope. Get over it. I'm here now. I'm here…with my daughter, with the whole family, okay? You don't have a right to question me, P." There was a silence after she spoke for about five seconds, and then she continued. "Just love me, Penelope. We're sisters and you're all I've got. You have to trust me."

"What was it…were you on drugs? What? What would have made you leave her on her own like that when she was only two years old, China? What? You keep too many damn secrets, and your husband was worried sick…"

"Penelope! Leave it alone!" China slammed the telephone down on the dashboard, causing Selah to stop humming.

"Are you and Aunt Penelope arguing again?" Selah asked. The light turned green, and the car in front of her started to move once again. China put the car back in drive.

"No…we aren't arguing again. Just talking…talking loudly. That's all. We're almost there." China pressed on the gas, and the car began to slowly accelerate behind the others. "I love you, Selah. I've never stopped, and I always will."

Selah started humming again, and in the meantime, China drove with tears streaming down her face. One of the hardest things that she'd ever had to do in her life was leave her home a couple years ago. Leaving her home meant leaving Selah as she slept in the middle of the night in her small bed while her dad slept in the other room. It was while she cleaned the kitchen that she got the idea to abandon her family for a while. Her purse sat on the kitchen table, and as she stroked the dirty counter with a bleached filled rag, she suddenly stopped. The pain in her side from her husband kicking her violently as Selah napped earlier that day continued to worsen until she had to swallow more pills to lessen her agony. He'd never hit her in the face, just her body, because he didn't want there to be any visible signs of how he would lose his temper and take it out on her. He was a police officer, and the job was stressful at times. China understood. This time was different, however. He stomped on her like she was a rag doll, and instead of walking out of the house like he normally would, Sean went into the bedroom, took a shower, got into the bed and slept. He did all this while she rolled in pain on the floor for an hour, and when she finally got up and looked into the mirror. Her face was totally the same – beautiful. Her spirit, mind and body were the exact opposite, however. They were all battered and broken. Without thinking any more, China took only her purse with her and left for one full month. It was Penelope who had to fix the broken pieces for China without a valid explanation as to why she abandoned Selah and Sean, mainly Selah. Penelope was clueless as everyone else, not knowing that her life at home wasn't so perfect, and Penelope had never forgiven her. She'd always believed the worst, not about the situation, but China.

By the time China found Penelope's new house, it was nearly two o'clock. This was Penelope's very first time moving into a place that she could call her very own, although it wasn't the nicest place. It was a bit run down, however, China knew that her sister was a go-getter, someone who would do all she could to make things the way she wanted them, that included this house.

"Get out of the car on this side, baby," China told Selah as she stepped out, feeling a sense of pride for her younger sister. It took her a while, but at least she could say that she earned every penny to support herself. When China tried to help her, Penelope always refused.

"Selah! Come up here and give your auntie a hug, girl! You're so big. Just in three weeks you look like a giant!" Penelope shouted as the screen door slammed behind her. There she stood on the front porch of her small, brick house as Selah ran to her like she was the only woman on earth. They were close, having grown their closest when China left for that short period of time that seemed like an eternity to them.

"Aunt Penelope!" Selah yelled as she ran to hop into her aunt's arms. China stood back about two feet in front of the car and smiled. Penelope returned the smile, closed her eyes and continued to hug Selah. Then, they all walked into the house, China entering last.

"You have it fixed up nicely in here, Penelope," stated China as she closed the door. "It looks great."

"Leave the door open, China, will you. I like the light to shine through the screen door. It saves on using electricity," she spoke coldly until finally speaking again. "Thank you. I learned something from mom, didn't I?"

"You sure did," China continued uneasily as she tipped further inside the living room while she watched Selah inspect everything in the house. "She knew how to decorate a house, and turn it into a home, didn't she?"

"Exactly, even when she had nothing. She always looked like she had everything."

China knew where the conversation was going ever since Penelope started talking about their mother. She and Penelope had different fathers because her mom married twice, but they never were close to their fathers. That left their mother as their rock when they were children.

Penelope stood there in the middle of the floor and finally invited China to sit down. "You can have a seat. The chairs don't bite. They aren't fancier than yours, but they still do the job and do the job quite well if you ask me…"

"Well, I didn't ask you, Penelope, did I?" China raised her voice as her daughter ran down the hallway to explore. There was a huge elephant in the room, and China was just about ready to slaughter it for good. "Just what is it with you, P? Aren't you a bit tired of maintaining this tension between us? No matter how hard I try, you just continue to break the peace."

"I didn't say one foul thing to you, China, so stop acting like the victim," Penelope stated as she walked over to the wall to straighten a picture frame.

"Penelope, I'm nobody's victim, and I'm sure as hell not acting like one. Drop this crap, okay?" China begged, frustrated and tired of the stone wall her sister had put up for two years.

"You're right. You're not the victim," she said, spinning around to face her sister eye to eye. "You've never been the victim, but mom…mom paid the price dearly. If anyone was a true victim of your sloppiness it was her."

"Penelope, shut up!"

"No! She saw you, China!"

A chill went down China's spine, and her fingertips seemed to get cold while her lip started to quiver. The words from Penelope's mouth hit her like a dagger to the heart as her thoughts fled from the present and went back to the past, a past that she'd already buried. Quickly, her eyes glanced toward the barren hallway and then back at her younger sister who stood strong, however, beneath all the strength were draperies of pain and hurt that fed into her defense. Tears began to flow down

88

China's eyes as she stood there, feeling as naked as she was when she would take her clothes off and swing around the pole before dozens of men each night.

"Yeah," Penelope continued as she stepped toward China. Tears rolled down her face as well while she continued speaking, "She came back home that night to me, China. I was worried sick because Mama wasn't ever out that late, and when she got in the house, she was breathing so hard. I remember it like it was yesterday. She fell onto the chair like she'd walked twenty miles in the hot sun, China, but it wasn't like that when I was able to see her face. She was crying the worst cry I'd ever seen, and when I looked down in her hand, she held a picture of you. It was all wet up in her tears, and I knew…I knew then," Penelope said wiping her eyes off with her wrists. "She'd seen you, China. So that's when I asked. I asked if she'd found you, and guess what she said?"

China only looked at her, suffering through the hurt being caused to her by Penelope's story. She wanted to run, but she couldn't because she'd already run from her troubles before making it difficult to up and leave again before her younger sister's eyes. Therefore, she stood there, taking the pain of what was coming next.

"I said guess, dammit!" The veins in Penelope's neck pulsated as she threatened China with her stance.

"I don't know, P!"

"She said that she'd found you swinging on a pole. She'd paid to get into the spot, and she was smirked at on the way inside by the doorman, especially when she asked him if he knew you. It was that smirk that told her you were in there. According to Mama, you were sliding down the top with your legs open until you hit the floor with your naked behind…"

Before Penelope got one more word out, China backslapped her into silence. Penelope lunged back at her, but China stopped her with one finger on her left hand and a balled up fist on the right. "Penelope, don't make me. Now, I know I wasn't the best daughter nor was I the best big sister, but I left okay? I left. I came back..."

"Yeah and after what? After mom died! She cried every night praying for you. Every single night, and it was only when she died that you got your senses and stopped strippin' and living like some whore! You killed her!"

China grabbed Penelope and pulled her into her body as tightly as she could. "I'm sorry, Penelope, I'm so sorry," she cried, sniffling on the shoulder of a stiffened Penelope. "I didn't know. You never told me, so I never knew. I didn't know she saw me, sis."

"Well, now you know. Top that off with the way you just left Selah with Sean when she was only two years old going to do God only knows what, I can see how you would feel just radiant now, huh?" Penelope stated sarcastically in China's ear, causing China to loosen her grip and back away. "You were never anything but a liability on an already bad day, China. You messed up mom's life just like you're messing up the family for Selah."

China looked down at her ribs, the same side that Sean kicked a dozen times the night she left her home, but instead of telling her sister about it, she remained silent. Deciding to take the blame and pain felt better than giving excuses because that was what she'd done all her life – made excuses. Besides that, no one would believe her. Her past was full of deceit as well as her present, just in different ways. She used to try to hide the disgrace of her past lifestyle, and as time went on, she also tried to hide behind the perfect façade of a family.

"The one thing you'll never know about me, Penelope, is the truth because you wouldn't believe the truth."

"Do you even have one?"

China wiped her eyes, cleared her throat, called for Selah, and when her daughter came up the hallway, she kneeled down to tell her that she would be back really soon to pick her up. Penelope only shook her head, remembering the days she took care of Selah while China was off doing whatever.

"Okay, Ma. I love you," she responded and gave her mother a kiss on the cheek before running back down the hallway.

"I love you, too, baby." Then, she looked back at Penelope. "I *will* be back to get her. I'm going to run some errands, but I will be back before you have to go to work." China then became like stone before warning Penelope of one thing, "Let's not talk about this again. You don't know what I do now or what I did nor the reasons why. All those days you and Ma had lights on in the house, I put that money on the bill. When you had running water, it was by my low down dirty ass that was swinging on that pole. I may not have been the best daughter or sister to you or Ma, I admit that, but I loved the both of you to death. Ma had no business seeing me on the pole…and you could have stopped her. I know you could have."

Penelope didn't move. "The lights may have been on, China, but I'd rather sit with a mother who is living in the pitch dark and cold than have to go every week to see her at the grave behind the heartache that you gave her. You killed her, and later you left Selah…what? To go get some bills paid on the pole again? I'd rather scrub toilets than hurt my family, but you don't know anything about that, do you? You're selfish. China, you left your own daughter!"

"You don't know! She doesn't remember! Leave it alone. I had my reasons, Penelope!" China stormed from the house and left the words of Penelope following her out.

"There's never any good reason for what you did to her or our mother!"

China nearly fell inside the car as the storm raging inside her exploded into a load of weeping onto the steering wheel. "He beat me, Penelope. Sean beat me. And your favorite Uncle Robert used to sleep with me when Ma was away. I had to leave!" she yelled, punching the dashboard until her hand bled from a small cut. "I had to go and try to make it on my own. I may have been selfish but I needed to be! I needed to be! I was tired of it!" China never had to strength to tell anyone about the abuse she'd endured, and she still continued to keep everything from her marriage quiet as she'd taught herself to do growing up. Besides, things were much better, and the façade was easier to deal with, for herself and others. By the time China left the front of her sister's house, her hand was throbbing.

Most Wanted Two

China had a favorite song titled *Spare Me the Details* that she would listen to all the time. It was that particular song that gave her the motivation to keep quiet despite what was said at her sister's house. She felt that sparing her younger sister the details would keep her from the terrible truth, and no matter what, she loved her enough to do that. Penelope was still her cute little sister in her eyes, and protecting her from everything was what she considered her duty, over protecting herself.

"Ouch," China complained about her hand as she opened the door to her spacious, suburban home. When she stepped inside, she immediately smelled cologne. "Sean?" she called, after kicking the door shut behind her and rushing over to the kitchen sink to rinse her hand off before bandaging it up with a band-aid that was in the First Aid kit. "Sean?" she called again, but got no answer.

She looked at the wall clock that hung on her freshly painted red accent wall, and it was past his normal lunch time. "I know he was home. He had to be." She reached down into her purse, grabbed her cell phone, and began to dial his number. There was no answer. It went straight to his voicemail.

She knew the smell of that cologne very well. It was his cologne of choice, and he only wore it when he wanted to impress. She liked to smell it on him as well. China tossed her purse onto the couch as she waltzed up the staircase, bypassing the garage. She was certain that he was somewhere in the house, possibly in the master bathroom, because the scent was so fresh.

93

I Will Do Anything For Her

As she turned into her bedroom, she called him again, "Sean, are you in the bathroom?" She walked over and knocked before turning the knob. Sean wasn't there. "He must have run in and out," she stated before noticing the leg of his uniform underneath the bed. She kneeled down until she could see completely under the bed, and to her surprise, Sean's entire uniform was laying there in one small pile with his work shoes.

A pit began to form in her stomach as she turned and fell against the bottom of the bed. China only sat there and stared at the bare ivory walls that sheltered her so many nights while she fought the worst battles of her lifetime. Tears began to flow down her cheeks as she reached for the landline phone that was on the nightstand beside her. She then dialed her husband's number again. Still, there was no answer. He was doing it again.

Moans began to take over her body as she rolled the back of her head back and forth against the mattress. Everything that she'd placed behind her in her life came back immediately, from Sean's long time affair to him even beating on her when she didn't meet his expectations and even the fresh argument with her sister who blamed her for everything under the sun, including their mother's death. It had been a long while since Sean laid a harmful finger on her, and she thought that he was changing. The sight of his clothes roughly handled under the bed and the smell of his best cologne told her that the beatings were about to start once again and really soon. This particular day, however, she didn't know how much more she could take.

China's thoughts took her back to the park where she met the woman named Raayna. Suddenly, China got up from the floor. She'd never in her life gone on a search to find the women her husband cheated on her with because it didn't matter. She'd only yearned for him to be honest and faithful to her. However and strangely enough, she wanted to know more about the

particular woman at the park, only because her child called Selah
sister.

Quickly, China got up from the floor, catching a glimpse
of the photo she took with Sean when he swore that he would
never hurt her again, and then headed down the staircase. She
counted the sound of her footsteps against the stairs as her mind
recalled the neighborhood where Raayna said she lived – Dew
Crossing. Another thing China tried to remember in detail was
how Raayna's daughter, Synthia, looked, but she couldn't.

Her hand continued to throb, so she reached into her
purse and took one more pain pill before heading out the front
door. Suddenly, she stopped, turning her attention toward the
garage. Sean usually left his car parked in the garage while his
squad car remained parked outside in the driveway next to hers.
If he'd gone back to work, his car would still be inside. If he
didn't, there would be a swap...as he'd been known to do before.

Slowly, she walked to door that led into the garage, took
a deep breath and opened it. There was the squad car, and her
heart sank deeper than what it had ever sank before. She knew.
He was cheating once again. All the phone calls to check on her
to see how she was doing during the day were just to find out if
she was at home or not...just like the one she got when she was
at the park with Selah. She'd been a fool again.

Instead of retracing her steps and moving back toward the
front door, she simply and quietly pressed the button that raised
the garage door and walked out. Then, she climbed inside her
car and drove away with a clear destination in mind.

Most Wanted Three

"I need to get a dozen roses…red roses. How long will that take, sir?" asked Sean as he stood at the counter, dressed in a casual beige shirt and brand new faded blue jeans.

"It won't take long. We already have some made up. Just a minute."

Sean nodded and glanced at his cell phone. It was his wife, China, however, he ignored the calls. Soon enough, the salesman came back out with a dozen roses to go with a beautiful card Sean had picked out. "Ahh, those will work," he sighed nervously.

"Must be a big day, huh?"

"You can say that," Sean responded.

"A proposal maybe?" the salesman asked after noticing that Sean had the jitters as well as noticing that there was no ring on his ring finger. "Don't worry about it," the older gentleman continued. "If she loves you, she'll say yes. If she doesn't, your mother will always deserve both the ring and the flowers. That's what I always said when I was at that stage in my life, son."

"Oh yeah?" Sean responded, playing the game.

"Sure," the man sighed. "A mom is always worthy. They work hard on us. Never a wasted flower."

"Great advice. Thanks." Sean paid for the flowers and card, and then he walked out of the shop, still a nervous wreck. When he arrived at his car that was only ten feet from the shop's entrance, he dropped the greeting card onto the street accidentally. Upon retrieving it, there was a small mark on the corner, but instead of going back inside to get another one, he simply wiped the card off the best that he could, got into the vehicle and drove off.

The music from the radio sounded off, but he quickly turned it down. He continuously repeated something over and over in a whisper, like it was a rehearsal. With every stoplight he came upon, he shifted in his seat, highly irritated yet determined to get what he had to get done completely finished. His cell phone rang again. It was China. He grabbed the cell phone and looked at her name and picture as the phone continued to ring. When he approached the next right turn, he placed the phone down carefully. Then, finally, it stopped ringing as he pulled into the driveway.

Prior to exiting the car, he made certain that his wedding ring was still in his pocket, and then without anymore hesitation, he opened the driver's side door. Before he got out, a little girl came running from the porch and into his arms.

"Hey, baby girl. Just the person I want to see," he stated, lifting her up from the cement.

"Hi, daddy. You came to take us out again?"

"Sure did. We're going somewhere special today."

"Can we ride in your car this time? I never get to ride in your car."

"Not this time. We're still taking your mom's car, honey."

"Synthia, come put on your shoes so we can go," called her mom as she slid on her wedged heels at the doorway. "Hey, baby," she smiled at Sean. "Almost ready…just give me two minutes."

Sean placed Synthia back down and watched her skip back to her mom who stood there with her shoes. Meanwhile, he quickly reached back into his car and placed a sports jacket atop the roses and card that he'd just bought. Then, he walked over to her car, sat inside the passenger's seat, and waited as he placed his cell phone on silent. In exactly two minutes, both Raayna and Synthia were on the way to the car.

In a restaurant they sat, all three of them, and they appeared happier than ever. During the drive, Raayna and Sean catered to Synthia's every demand as they normally did when they went out. Whatever Synthia wanted to sing, they sang. Whatever sounds she wanted to make, they made along with her. Things went well on the ride and as they sat down to eat. The only thing that was different was the way Sean felt, and as the day turned to evening, Raayna noticed.

"What's going on, Sean? Hard day?" She'd noticed that his hands stayed beneath the table, and on any other usual date, one of his hands would be stretched across the table joining with hers.

"A little bit, but nothing that I couldn't handle. Had a couple of hard knocks that got arrested early this morning, but that comes with the job. How about you? How was your day?"

Raayna pretended as if she didn't hear the question by asking her daughter to spread the napkin out over her lap so the food wouldn't spill onto her clothing.

"Raayna, did things go well for you?"

"Oh yeah, they did. We…uh…went to hang out a bit. Play around outside…"

98

"Yeah, dad, we went to the park, and I met…"

Before Synthia even got the words out of her mouth, Raayna reached up with a smile on her face and spilled her tea all over Synthia's food and clothes. "Oh goodness, Synthia, get up, honey. Get up and let's go to the bathroom. Sean, will you take care of this? I can't believe I did that."

"No, no, I got it. Are you okay, baby girl?" he asked his daughter.

"I'm all wet," she cried.

"It'll be okay. Let's go to the bathroom and fix you up again, okay? Mama's sorry."

"Okay," Synthia whined.

Raayna walked as calmly as she could to the women's restroom, and when she got there, she not only waited on a stall, but she also waited on everyone to leave. That was when she pulled off many paper towels and spoke to Synthia.

"Synthia, baby, I thought I told you that you shouldn't tell your dad who you met today. Didn't I mention that to you?" she asked as she wiped her down.

"Yes ma'am," she dragged. "I just wanted him to know that I met my sister."

"I know you did, but you don't want to do that yet, okay? Let me tell him some things before you do that. Deal? And if you let me tell him first, I promise you that I will get you whatever present you want."

"Deal. My mouth is zipped."

She leaned in and kissed her on the cheek. "That's my good girl. Now come on, let's go. Remember, no telling," Raayna smiled but inside she was a nervous wreck. She promised herself that she would hold it together however, and that was exactly what she did. On the way back to the table, she behaved as if all was fine, but deep on the inside, she knew she did exactly what Sean didn't want her to do – approach China.

"Is everything all better, my little ray of sunshine?" Sean asked his little girl as she hopped onto his lap.

"Yep, daddy. I'm still a little bit wet though." She then looked to onto the table. "Oh, it's already all clean!" She jumped down from his lap and went back to her seat. "I'm ready to finish eating."

Raayna kept her eyes lowered as she'd already started to feast on the food that was before her, and when she noticed Sean's uneasy appearance, she felt that he'd figured out that she'd done the one thing that would set him off. Instead of confessing, she still maintained her silence about the matter although there was massive tension at the table.

Sean didn't utter a word although he was barely eating his meal. He continuously clasped his fingers together as if he was in prayer, while inconspicuously and repeatedly looking at his bare ring finger. As he stared at who he considered a beautiful woman in Raayna – nice, flawless skin and the perfect figure to add to the impulsiveness and radiance of her personality that continued to lead him to curiousity – she wasn't who he wanted anymore. Staring at her in all his infatuation, he'd realized months ago that he truly wasn't in love with her. Raayna wasn't the woman he wanted to be with at all. He still loved his wife, and if he'd divorced China the next day, he truly felt that he would grow tired of Raayna because all she was when stripped down was nice, naughty and naked. He needed more.

He'd made another terrible, emotional decision…but this one came with a child.

For months, he'd been proving to China he was a better man, and never lifted a finger to her since that last time he'd hit her. The only thing that wore on him was the fact that he continued to see Raayna, which was only to figure out what his next move would be that would allow him to remain with his wife while at the same time telling her that Selah had a sister. Time passed, and he could figure nothing out. Sure, he felt like he owed Raayna and Synthia better, but he also felt like he owed China and Selah a whole lot more because this second family was never supposed to happen. Tonight was the night, and Sean desperately wanted to be a changed man…for the better.

After finishing their late lunch date, the ride was quiet on the way back to Raayna's home. They barely spoke a word to each other, and if it weren't for the singing and laughter of Synthia, there would have been nearly complete silence. Sean sat up the whole way back, which was abnormal. A reclined state was generally best for him, especially after he'd eaten a meal because he'd want to relax. He was a fairly built man with a dark-brown, flawless complexion. His facial structure was built like that of a male fashion model, one with a strong cheek bone and deeply set dark-brown eyes. Sean didn't have to do much to himself to attract the attention of any woman, but it had been months since he'd wanted the attention of any other woman but his wife.

"Let me go put Synthia to bed for a nap. She's already dozing off," Raayna stated as she put the car in park after pulling up beside his car in the driveway. "I'll be right back…because it's obvious that something is going on. I don't want to talk about anything in front of or around Synthia, so just wait in the car, okay?"

Sean didn't dispute her. He knew exactly where she was coming from, and he knew his portion of the conversation was going to be something he definitely didn't want his daughter to hear being that she was the inquisitive type. Sean closed his eyes and attempted to rehearse all he had to say in his mind, but before he could even say it aloud, there was Raayna walking back toward the car. Then, she opened the door and got inside.

Staring straight ahead, almost like she knew what was coming, she finally asked him, "What?"

"Raayna," he started, but she cut him off with tears in her eyes. Sean stalled.

"What, Sean? I know my name, so don't say it again," she said holding back tears. "Tell me...what?" she asked, but Sean, instead of saying anything immediately, he simply took her by the hand.

Most Wanted Four

There she sat at the side of the road on the corner inside the neighborhood called Dew Crossing. After driving around the neighborhood for some time, she finally saw her husband's car parked at a home that appeared well kept …by a woman. On the porch were pink and yellow potted flowers, and there was also a rather large potted plant with tropical leaves. Hanging above them was a colorful chime that, when the wind blew, shook violently as if it weighed next to nothing. Then, a car pulled into the driveway, and she watched a woman and child exit.

China's heart plummeted as she watched the woman she'd met earlier that day at the park walk into the house along with her daughter that she remembered was named Synthia. There was another body inside the car, sitting in the passenger's seat. It took no time for her to trace her husband's outline as she watched him shuffle around in the car, and she was almost surprised that he didn't see her staring directly at him. Almost in a daze, she watched as the woman she knew as Raayna walk back outside to sit inside the car with Sean. There was nothing left to see after she watched Sean lean in toward the woman that sat in the driver's seat and give, what China deemed, a kiss to his mistress. She turned the car around and left.

The traffic appeared all a blur as China drove through town back to her home. In the back of her mind, she knew that she had to pick up Selah from her sister's home soon, however, there was going to be a problem with doing that. Her emotions were weighing her down, and for the first time in her life, through all the cheating and fighting, she felt like she could kill her own husband.

A traffic light turned red and China ran through it, being caught up in her erupting feelings. She'd actually started learning to love him again because over the past several months, Sean had been nothing but exemplary, making it easier for her to laugh through the pain that he'd caused her. To find that it was all a lie devastated China so much so that running that red light was almost a plea for someone to take her away from it all. She'd heard people say that once your heart got broken by someone, that same someone couldn't break your heart again. They were right. China's heart wasn't broken as much as it was drowning in betrayal.

As she turned down her street, neighbors waved, but she didn't wave back. She then pulled the car onto the freshly cleaned driveway, stepped out, and finally entered her home through the front, placing her purse down at the door. China immediately went into the master bathroom to take a hot shower. She'd always liked her showers extremely hot. Sean couldn't stand it that way, and when they would take showers together, she hated how he would create a lukewarm temperature. For months, however, she'd started enjoying sharing the shower with Sean because it was just like when they first married.

A stroke of pain hit her heart as the water fell upon her face and hair as a flash of Sean being with Raayna came to her mind. Her gut was correct when she stalled at the park. The water continued to roll down her back as she grew stiff at the thought of Raayna purposely approaching her at the park with Synthia. It was obvious to China that Raayna had already told her daughter that Selah was her sister, and China's rage started to grow intense. She wanted to do something horrible to Raayna, not for sleeping with her husband, but for befriending her as if all was great. The deception became too much to bear, so she exited the shower. Before she dried off, however, she ended up standing there, inspecting herself in the mirror.

Her hair was always like he told her he loved it, full of her natural curls that draped her shoulders. The reflection of her skin in the mirror mingled with the mist with perfection because one of the one things she'd learned from her former days as a stripper was how to keep her skin and body nice, smooth and toned. That's what the men liked to see, and that was what her husband loved to touch…at least that was what she thought.

She began to think about how she would have dinner cooked for him every night, something that Raayna never had to do to please him. Sean's clothes would always be neatly ironed or dry cleaned, and it wasn't because she had to do it. It was only because the last several months, he'd appeared to be going above and beyond. Finally, one tear rolled down her face. The nice smiles and caresses at night that she'd started to fall back in love with were all a great gimmick, to keep her deceived in the worst way, and China suddenly felt that he'd beat her all over again.

Instead of continuing on in the mirror, she blotted her skin dry, rubbed coconut oil over the tops of her feet, smoothed Shea Butter on the rest of her skin, and wiped a tea cloth across her face. She then walked into her bedroom and began packing a bag. It was her favorite bag to pack whenever she went out of town, and although she had no destination in mind, she felt she needed to pack and pack lightly.

Her sneakers were tucked partially underneath the nightstand, and without socks, she slid her feet inside. China also grabbed some panties, soap, lotion and a light jacket along with her other items, sectioned them nicely inside the bag, and zipped it up. She then walked to the closet and grabbed a shoebox. From there, she combed through her hair with her fingers as it was starting to curl back up to her shoulders, and she wrapped a band around the bottom of it in order to stop the curl at that length. Finally, she put on some jeans and a white crop top, gathered her gear, and went to the bottom of staircase…to sit down.

From her purse, which she left at the front door, she saw her cell phone's light blinking. She knew who it was. It had to be Penelope. It had been two hours since she dropped Selah there to spend time with her, and it was time for China to pick her up in fifteen minutes. It wasn't going to happen.

There was a chocolate candy bar in her bag. She kept them in the room because that was her favorite snack before she fell asleep. It wasn't a full sized candy bar; just a small one to curb her appetite during the night. She slowly opened the wrapper, paying attention to the way she unwrapped it in detail, careful not to rip one piece of the perfectly designed foil. When the candy bar was completely uncovered, she heard a car pull into the driveway. China didn't move. Instead, she continued to chew on the candy bar as she placed her hand atop the shoebox. Upon hearing the keys at the front door, she uncovered the brown and black shoebox and retrieved a pistol. As the door came open, she swallowed the last of her candy bar, rubbed the chocolate from her fingers on her blue jeans while placing the pistol carefully behind her back. She watched as her husband walked in. He was stunned to see her on the staircase.

"China…hi, baby," he greeted her immediately with a warm smile, as if he'd never been engaging with another woman and his other child. She watched him glance down to shut and lock the door behind him, and when he did, she aimed the pistol directly at his chest.

"Are those flowers for me?" China questioned as she placed her finger on the trigger. She watched intently as Sean's body froze at the door, flowers in his left hand along with a greeting card. His frozen stance suddenly changed into one of a guilty man, and China could tell by the look on his face that he already knew he was caught.

"China," he sighed like all hope in the world was gone as his eyes planted down on her trigger finger. "Please…baby…I'm sorry. Look, I got you some…"

China pulled the trigger because she simply didn't want to hear what he had to say. When the bullet hit him in the chest, his knees locked, and he went silent. She didn't even wait for his body to fall to the floor before she got up. He stared directly at her from his weakened body that finally fell to the floor as she stood up from the staircase and walked over to him. She knew that he kept another pistol at his ankle, so she stepped on his wrist to keep him from reaching for it. Instead of looking at him, she leaned down and took the roses and greeting card from his hand. When she felt his body go limp, she callously smelled the roses that she knew he gathered to cover his cheating. Then, she dumped them over onto his body.

Finally, she removed her foot from his wrist that she'd pinned down and slid down the front door until she came to a seated position beside his body. She began to cry for the first time as she watched his body lie there on the floor next to the card that she would have taken from him, believing that it was full of love.

"You son of a bitch!" she screamed as she kicked her husband's dead body as hard as she could. "I hate you! You fuck around on me and our daughter!" She took a deep breath, and then her stiffened body went limp with emotional pain as she continued, "And you gave her a sister by another woman. Did you even know she talked to me today? Huh? You…I hate you!" She kicked him again and then picked up the greeting card. "Is this supposed to be your fucked up way of telling me you love me? Had me believing your ass this time. Now, how the fuck does it feel?" she asked again, kicking him in his stomach the way he kicked her years ago. "So, you want me to read this shit?" she asked, tossing it over into her purse which was slightly open.

Her anger boiled over, but it didn't overtake the panic that she'd placed herself in with the knowledge that she'd shot not only her husband but an officer of the law. Quickly, she snatched up her purse along with the roses that he'd bought her, stuffed them inside the handbag, grabbed the bag of clothing and left him dying on the floor. She had to move, and move fast.

His patrol car was located inside the garage, and that was the way she decided to exit because it was the quickest route to her car. Before tapping the switch that would cause the garage door to open, China took four deep breaths. Her breathing had become sporadic, and she could tell her blood pressure was escalating. On the third breath, she thought about her daughter, whether or not she should go and pick her up from Penelope's and pretend like nothing ever happened. On the fourth breath, she knew that if she picked up her daughter, Selah would end up watching her mother on the run, and she wouldn't understand…not that it could be understood. Selah would have no where stable to go, and China knew, based off being married to a cop, that she couldn't even go to the bank to get money. There would be the potential for a trace by police everywhere she went, including on her cell phone.

"Where is it, where is it?" she asked herself frustrated as she dropped the items in the garage and searched her purse. Once she found her cell phone, she turned it completely off, saddened all the way through to her soul that she wouldn't be able to see or talk to her daughter anymore, at least for a while. "I love you, Selah," she continued, choking back the tears for her daughter that she couldn't shed for Sean. She turned back to the door that led back inside her home only once, and when everything fell silent outside, she hit the garage switch and daylight slowly entered. Finally, the garage door opened.

Most Wanted Five

"You like this room?"

"Auntie Penelope, this room is great! Is this where I'm supposed to come all the time and play?" Selah asked jumping on all the stuffed animals.

"When you come and spend the weekends with me, it's all yours. I will fix it up just for you. When you're gone, I will tuck all this stuff away nice and neat for you when you come back."

"This is my bed, too?"

"When you come over it is," Penelope laughed.

"Aunt Penelope, when are you gonna have a baby so I can have a cousin?"

Penelope got silent. There was no way that she could have babies since everything was removed due to cancer. Penelope didn't want to take the risk of anything spreading, so she elected to have her reproductive organs removed. This was another reason she loved Selah so much. It was because deep down inside, she knew that Selah was going to be the only child close to a daughter that she would ever have. Penelope was going to make the most of it.

"I'll try, sweetheart, but first Auntie Penelope has to get married to the right man. I can't come rolling up to my house with a baby with no way to feed it, now can I? All my money is going to this house and you right now," she lied.

"Me?"

"You'll lose this room if I have a baby, now won't you?"

"We can share! She can have this side and I can have this side," Selah stated, pointing to each half of the bedroom.

"Well," Penelope sighed and looked around, "I'll think about it. In the meantime, get ready to go. Your mom should be coming around the corner any minute. I'll see you next week, okay? And then, we can have a slumber party with some of the other little girls I know from my old neighborhood."

"Okay," Selah responded happily. "I can't wait to ask mom."

Penelope walked to the living room and peeked out of the window. When she saw no sign of China, she sat on the couch and thumbed through a magazine while Selah put her shoes on in the back room. Thirty minutes turned into an hour, and there was still no sign of China. Penelope was pacing the floor by then, pretending that everything was alright when something in her gut told her that things were all wrong...again.

She glanced at her cell phone every five minutes, and she even placed it back on the charger to be certain that it was charged up. Still, she got no feedback from China after having already called her phone many times. Her calls were continuously answered by voicemail. It was almost time for her to get ready to work a night shift at the store, so she had no choice but to call Sean, however, when she did, she still received no answer.

By that time, Selah was already sitting on the couch watching Penelope pace back and forth, until she finally sat down. Tears began to well up in her eyes as she watched Selah continue to peep out of the blinds for her mother. Her thoughts raced back to the first time Selah was abandoned, and there was a horrible sense that crept beneath her skin, telling her that this was the second time that her sister China was leaving.

Penelope felt sick, so she raced to the bathroom to quickly remove herself from Selah's line of vision. As soon as she stood in front of her freshly cleaned toilet, she vomited. When she caught her breath, she placed the lid down on the seat, sat down, and dialed her job. Her nerves were brutally disturbed because she'd just changed jobs, and this particular job was her best one yet. The pay was more than enough to pay her bills and even have some left for a movie night and dinner along with a trip to the spa. With each ring of the phone, however, Penelope felt like her dreams were going to fall apart due to her older sister once again.

"Hello. Hi, it's Penelope Greenwater. I realize that I am to be at work soon, and I just wanted to give you the heads up that I may end up running late. This isn't typical, but I am going to end up fighting traffic due to a problem ... with my car." She paused to listen to the person on the other end speaking before she continued again with her lie. "I got into a car accident, and I can bring you in the ticket as proof. Just waiting on the officer to arrive. No..." she paused again as she thought about the old traffic ticket that she had tucked away somewhere in her purse. "I'm fine. I just can't leave at the moment, so I will see you later when I get there?" she asked, unsure if everything would be okay. "Thanks."

Penelope burst into tears after hanging up the telephone, not just because of her job being on the line due to the fact that she had no idea what to do with Selah but for the feeling she couldn't shake. Something was terribly wrong. She had a sick sense, and it wouldn't leave her alone.

I Will Do Anything For Her

After leaving the bathroom, she raced into her bedroom and turned over her purse. Everything fell out, from her wallet, packs of chewing gum and even her car keys wrapped in a couple of grocery store receipts. Penelope, then, opened her purse wide and searched for the one piece of paper she had to have in order to pull this lie off at work.

"Come on. Every time I open my purse, you're there, and when I ..." she continued but stopped when she found it. "Yes!"

There was a pen sitting on the night stand beside her bed, and she quickly grabbed it to etch the correct date on the ticket in order to pass it off as being written as of that day. Then, she immediately wiped the tears from her eyes, loaded her purse back up with the things she'd emptied out, and went into the living room to see Selah.

"Sweetheart, do you see your mom out there anywhere?" she asked already knowing the answer because she was staring out the window from behind her.

"No ma'am, I don't."

"Well, you're coming with me. We're going to go meet your mom at your house, okay?"

"Okay!" Selah responded excitedly.

"Are you ready to go?"

"Sure am!"

"Well, let's go, baby," Penelope responded trying to sound upbeat, but hoping and praying that someone would be at home when she got there. There was no way she was going to leave Selah with anyone of her neighbors or their neighbors for that fact, so the only alternative to get to her job in time was to drive Selah home. They entered the car and left.

Most Wanted Six

"I need to talk to Jayce," China explained after driving to the strip club where she used to make lots of money. "He knows exactly who I am, so don't look at me like that," she continued, looking behind herself to force the door shut. She'd parked around the back side of the club in order to avoid being spotted by anyone, or for that matter, any police officers. She was certain that at this particular time, no one had found out that Sean was dead. China was smart about her next moves though, being a woman who was fairly familiar with living on the streets. She didn't want to go to the ATM machine to pull out money because it would allow the police to track her moves, and all she had on her was a couple hundred dollars. She needed more for herself and also Selah.

It was Friday, and the club was going to be packed. China needed to get back on stage to make some money as quickly as possible. She glanced up at the posters that lined the club that featured one of the hottest artists in the city, and this particular artist always brought an entourage with enough money for every girl to make at least two or three months mortgage. China didn't want to do it, but she had no choice. She knew that her body looked the same as it did back then or even better.

"What's your name?" the attendant asked as she looked China over while holding the phone to her ear. There was no way that China was going to give her true identity, so she barked loudly back at the woman who was only trying to do her job.

"Jayce, it's me! I left...but now I'm back. I need to talk to you. Needs, baby, needs." "*Needs, baby, needs*" were the

three words that she and Jayce used to laugh about when she
would count her dollars at the end of the night. China would
always work so hard during sets until Jayce would always go to
the back to see her and laugh. China would respond with
"Needs, baby, needs" to let him know that she was doing it for
good reasons. She would tell him everything about those needs
although he never asked. He would also never judge her reasons.
She would just pay him his cut, and she would leave with the
cash.

Before China could blink three times, there was Jayce
coming through the swinging double doors that led into the main
floor of the club. He was wearing all white, from the jeans to the
shirt and shoes. He'd gone from the Rastafarian look to a
smooth, low cut fade and a go-tee that was barely there. He
stopped in his tracks when he saw China looking the exact same
way as when she stopped dancing. China's hair was still wet
from the shower she took, but it draped with fullness down to her
shoulders. Her light brown skin shown to be flawless as usual,
and when Jayce walked over to her, he reached out his hand and
led her back to his office.

There was one thing that many people didn't know at the
club. Jayce and China were once a item. As she walked back,
she remembered the days when they would connect back in this
same office, and as soon as Jayce closed the door of his office
behind her, it was obvious that he'd remembered as well. He
walked up behind her closely, however, when China felt the
warmth from his body, she didn't feel the same warmth. Instead,
she felt cold, and she quickly moved away, turning to face him.

"It's not like that, Jayce. I'm married," she stuttered with
a flashback of her dead husband, "but thanks for seeing me."

"I know you're married. Still on top of things though," he stated as he looked her body over. China noticed and decided to cut off his stare with her words.

"I need to dance tonight, Jayce. Don't call me by my name though. Call me something else, but not China. I see you're going to have a good crowd here tonight."

"But you're not that main girl anymore, China. It's been years. Nobody knows you. You think you can get up there, married and all, and give the same thing you used to give when it was me and you?" He leaned over on his desk. "What's your man got to say about that? I know if you were my wife…"

"Well, I'm not, Jayce, and like I said…I have needs. Besides that, my husband doesn't know," China stated looking away. "And I need to be out there when most of the money is seated."

"You askin' for a lot, China," he responded as he watched a tear fall from her eye. He quickly moved toward her and pulled out the money he generally carried on him. "China, baby, I'm not hardcore like that. I got love for you. Another girl was already requested for that VIP I know you're talking about though, and …"

"Put your money back, Jayce, because it's not enough. You owe me! You're gonna always owe me!" China yelled, tears streaming down her face. Then, she calmed down as she watched Jayce put the money back in his pocket. "Trust me, Jayce, I don't want to do this, but I have to. I need to get outta here. Do what you have to do, but get me that section."

Disturbed by her desperation, Jayce knew she was in trouble. It wasn't like China to appear at a loss or begging for that matter because he'd always seen her put together well, even when she had absolutely nothing. China was always able to put on a nice front when her back was up against the wall, but this time, Jayce felt in the pit of his stomach that he needed to extend the favor, especially for all she'd done for him in the past.

"Look, I have some time. Let me go drop some lines, make you the girl they want tonight, and that's all I can do. If you're the girl that they want in VIP, then all that money is in your pocket," he stated. "I tell you what though. This must be something bad, China," he sighed as he walked to the door. "Last time I saw you, you wanted to change your life, live for the Lord and all that, get married and have a family. Now you're back here?"

"Just for one night," she said wiping her eyes.

"Why don't you just let me handle whatever you need?" he asked, still having a great deal of feelings for the woman that stood before him.

"Because it comes with a price, Jayce. Don't you live by that still? A freebie means a freebie?" she responded sternly. "Like I said, you don't have enough. I can earn it, just like I've done hundreds of times before."

"Be back at midnight," he responded.

"Yeah…just one thing about that "*be back at midnight*". I need to stay here. Right here, inside your office. I can't leave until I make all my money." At her words, Jayce walked over to his chair and had a seat. China cringed at what might come next. She wasn't his girl anymore, and that meant he was going to be as fair as he ever was with anyone. That type of fair meant his way or no way, but she was surprised by the next words that came from his mouth which proved he still had a soft spot for her.

"You know I have a place right here for you," he stated, pointing to his chest. "I always will. When you let that man go, you know where to find me. Crash right here until the morning. I have something for you to wear in the drawer right here. Brand new, too. I know you don't do that swapping shit."

"Got something to eat?" she asked with a relieved smile on her face, grateful that he'd been so nice to her after all the time they spent apart. Jayce could be a handful for anyone, and she was happy to know that he was still on her side, the same as she used to be for him.

"Damn, China," he laughed. "Hold tight. I'll grab you something. You better kill it tonight. This is a real freebie." He walked over and kissed her on the cheek. "You know I got love for you, and I don't wanna know shit. Just dance." He walked around her, and China grabbed his arm.

"Thanks, Jayce." She watched him walk out the door, and once he did, she locked it behind him, sat on his chair and cried. She knew it was only going to be a little bit more time before someone found out that Sean was dead, and she would never be able to hold her daughter in her arms again.

Most Wanted Seven

Penelope knocked on the door after pulling into the driveway of her sister's home. It was luscious compared to her home. China had an arched doorway made of the perfect color brick, and the landscape of the front yard was crafted to marvel each week. Every house on the block reflected amazing, but Penelope wasn't concerned about appearances at all this day. She was more concerned about keeping her brand new way of life up the best way she could, and that was by keeping her job.

"China," she called through the door, but after waiting there for about one full minute, there was still no answer. Her phone calls continued to go unanswered, and even when she called for Sean, despite the visibility of his car right beside hers in the driveway, he didn't answer the door or phone either.

"What is this stupid code?" Penelope whispered to herself as she approached the garage. "She told me this thing a hundred times already. Let me see…" she stated as she lifted the cover to the garage's keypad. On the first try, nothing happened, and then, Penelope started to get nervous. She didn't want anyone to think she was trying to break inside, so she waved to Selah to get out of the car. The fact that Selah was outside in plain view would alert the neighbors to things being fine if they were taking notice.

"Selah, do you know this code by any chance, baby?"

"No ma'am. I can't reach it anyway."

"Yeah, you're right," she answered, dialing in another set of numbers for the fourth time. To her amazement, the garage door started to move. "Yes," she sighed. "Come on. Let's go in here and see where your mom is...or for that matter, your dad. Both his cars are here, but apparently, he's not."

It was common knowledge to both Selah and Penelope that if the garage door was down, the door into the house from the garage was open. Sean and China did that just in case either one of them got locked out. If everyone was inside the house, the back door would typically be locked. Therefore, Penelope turned the knob, and the door came open.

"Hello! Don't shoot, people. It's me, Penelope. I need to drop Selah back off here," she said loudly. She, then, motioned Penelope in the house where she immediately ran into the kitchen, opened a drawer and pulled out a piece of candy her dad always hid for her. As Penelope entered, she walked beyond the kitchen and as soon as she turned the corner, she released a horrific scream. Bolting to hide Selah from the scene, she pushed her back out into the garage and ordered her to sit down. Selah began crying as a result of her aunt's forcefulness, but she sat still as she watched her aunt run back into the house.

"Jesus," she cried, grabbing the wall as she nearly collapsed at the sight of Sean on the floor right in front of the front door. She was about to run toward him, but she stopped, afraid of who may be inside the house when her main priority was protecting Selah. Even worse, she was afraid for her sister. "China! China!"

Grabbing her cell phone she fumbled through dialing the only three numbers she needed to dial to get help – 911. Her breathing grew faint as she imagined her sister inside the home somewhere dead or having been taken somewhere and killed because her car wasn't at home. Penelope began to sob even worse when the operator answered on the other end of the phone after her thoughts took her to every place that wasn't good.

"Hello, send somebody here please. My brother in law is a cop, and he is on the floor just lying there, and his chest isn't moving. It isn't moving!" she screamed. "I just got here and walked in, and I don't know where my sister is…somebody…oh Jesus no," she stated, collapsing on the floor. From the corner of her eye, she saw Selah running her way, but she frantically waved her arm and shouted, "Go back, Selah! Sit down I said and stay there!" Selah cried in horror once again because her aunt had never yelled at her before. She was terrified, so terrified that she ran out of the garage. Penelope jumped up and ran after her, catching her at the edge of the driveway. Selah was screaming and hollering, alerting the neighbors so much until they ran out of their houses to come to her rescue. Penelope got on her knees with tears covering her face and held her tightly.

"It's gonna be fine, baby. Auntie is sorry for yelling, but you can't go inside the house. There might be something dangerous in there. I'm so sorry."

"You scared me, Aunt Penelope," Selah cried, hugging her aunt back as she listened to her talk on the phone.

"Yes, please, send the cops and an ambulance right now. Please…" Penelope continued as she watched more and more people surround her on the driveway. All she could do was hold her niece and weep. The police and ambulance arrived within ten minutes, and by the beginning of nightfall Selah was placed in the care of Penelope, while never finding out what it was that happened to her father inside the house.

Most Wanted Eight

The music blasted as loudly as it could get in the club, and Jayce had provided China with something great to wear for the crowd that she was to entertain. China was slightly nervous about the night because she still hadn't seen anything about the shooting on television as of the eleven o'clock news. It was nearing twelve, and instead of waiting to see whether or not she should change her facial features with make-up, she decided to anyway, just in case she ended up on the television screen. There would be plenty people in the crowd, and she couldn't chance it.

There was a load of makeup in the bag that she packed, so she started to transform into the woman she used to be. She contoured her nose which made it appear slimmer, and she glazed her eyelids and placed on fake eyelashes to make her eyes appealing while her foundation and powder changed her complexion slightly, giving her a browner tone. By the time she finished piling on the makeup and fluffing out her hair, the contour of her face wasn't a dead giveaway for anyone...unless they alrcady kncw her. There should not have been any dancer at the club that could make her out because it had been over ten years since she danced, and most people she knew had already moved on. This would work to her advantage.

As time winded down, she prepared to keep her head down and walk down the hallway. Before she walked out the door, Jayce unlocked the door and walked inside. There she stood, fully dressed to undress and ready to go, and Jayce still liked what he saw.

"I see you're ready, but why all that big of a change? You look better without that little ass nose," he teased. "You don't want anyone to recognize you, do you?"

"Obviously, Jayce. Thanks, too."

"You got that VIP. Just go out there, and do your thing. They just came through the door. Let the drinks come, and when the money starts flyin', turn it up. He's over there waiting on you, so don't make us look bad, baby girl. You know his pockets are deep," he stated pertaining to the celebrity that he'd obviously convinced somehow to request her.

There was a deep silence, and neither one of them knew what else to say. It was awkward for China because she didn't know why Jayce was staring at her like he had something important to tell her. Finally, the mood changed when he opened his mouth.

"You know I checked things out about you. I can't have heat come down on me without knowing what to do or say in order to look out for you."

China only looked away. She knew he would end up investigating things, but the code for Jayce was that he never wanted to know facts. He always wanted to put things together on his own because he wasn't a snitch. What he didn't know for a fact, he couldn't say to police under assumption.

"What did you find out…about me?"

"It's big. More than that, you have to get out of town. There are bugs crawling all around your house. You need some fog, if you understand what I'm saying. Things aren't hot yet, but by sun up, those bugs will be everywhere. I've never seen so many. People are talking."

I Will Do Anything For Her

Before China became too upset to work, she walked around him and out of the door. She didn't need to hear anymore. All she needed to do was make the money she needed and leave town…after getting some money to Selah and Penelope. After that, she could bounce from club to club easily and make money at any city in the country without the police tracking her. She planned to go as far out west as her body could take her and then make her rounds from the north and east. She would have to leave the south behind. She'd already resolved to send cash inside a card each time she was leaving a city, and that money would land in Penelope's mailbox. There was no way Penelope would turn her in to the authorities, but she felt that Penelope wouldn't protect her either. She was on her own, and she knew it.

When it was time to dance, she took a deep breath, shut her eyes, and imagined she was dancing for one million dollars before a crowd of people who were watching her on a movie screen. She prepared herself to feel the money touching her as she allowed her thoughts to take her to a standing ovation, believing the money was actually roses. Before, when she was younger, she would have to get nearly drunk to strip and dance before a crowd of men. Tonight, she needed to be sober, just in case she was identified and singled out by an undercover cop.

China opened her eyes as she slid down the pole and found her source of much money. It took no time for her to grab a seat on the celebrity's lap and make him feel extra special. She felt the money going into her straps, and when she took one of the bills inside her mouth, she saw exactly what she wanted to see. They were fifty dollar bills. He was one of the biggest spenders, and he always wanted a good show. China gave him what he paid for. As the singles fell, all he tossed her way were fifties and hundreds. She wasn't going to move. All of her energy went on him, and as the other girls came out, she didn't share her spot. He was her man, and she was his lady. She had needs for her daughter, and they would be met.

Suddenly and as China was turning back around to face her personal celebrity client, he leaned in to her face and whispered something into her ear. His hand went around her neck, and she continued to dance, not knowing what he was doing initially. However, when his lips touched her ear, she heard him loud and clear over the music.

"A friend of mine told me you were worth more than most tonight. He didn't lie."

China continued to dance as if she didn't hear anything he said. She wasn't in the business of striking deals with customers or making much conversation because it always led to nothing she wanted to do. Everything she danced for, she wanted and needed to feel she earned it, not begged or laid on her back for it. Therefore, she wasn't going to allow any conversation between herself and this particular client. When everything ended, she'd made more money than any of the girls around her, and they knew it. They chased singles while she made larger notes, and the bills easily made a thick belt all around her waist and in her bra, minus her fistfuls.

It took China no time to walk back to the hallway with all her cash. She wasn't fazed by all the dirty looks she was given by the girls who felt she shouldn't have been there, but they didn't know China's history with the club. There was a time when she was all people came to see, and she earned that reputation. Absolutely nothing was given to her, and of that, she was proud.

As she started removing the money from her body, she stalled in her gait as a woman stopped directly in front of her. Without looking up, China said, "Excuse me," but the woman didn't move. China then moved the other way in order to slide by her, however, when she looked up, she thought she'd seen a ghost. It was Raayna, and she was ready to dance.

For a moment, they both just stared at each other. China didn't expect to see her, and it was obvious that Raayna didn't expect to see China as she scanned China's body that held nothing less than hundreds of dollars. Before her eyes even made it back up to meet China's, she was taken in tears running down her face.

"So, I heard you used to do this, but I didn't think…" Raayna started as she wiped the tears from her eyes, taking her make-up with them.

"Who did you hear that from?" China stated in an attempt to sound like she had no idea that her husband was having an affair with the woman standing right in front of her. "And I don't do this…"

Raayna started to laugh, interrupting China. "Well, what's this?" She snatched money from China's strap. "I knew about you already, China," she continued, as the tears ran down her face even faster than what they did only seconds ago, confusing China who just stood there, afraid of what Raayna might know due to all the crying. "Me and Sean were still having our affair, even after the first time you found out about another woman. That woman was me," she sniffled. "And we have a baby," she confessed through her tears while the words struck China to her heart, but she didn't move, desperately afraid to let on that she knew anything about the affair. "I met you at the park today so Synthia could meet her sister behind Sean's back. You could say I had inside intel to know you would be there," she stated sarcastically but then suddenly became serious once again. "I felt you deserved to know, but I couldn't tell you everything, so I didn't. I should have though, because me and Sean ain't together anymore." Raayna's voice shook as she spoke, barely able to get the words out. "He still loves you, so I guess you won…if there is such a thing since he was always your husband. Not mine."

As Raayna stood there crying, China nodded her head, moved around Raayna, and continued down the hallway. She felt Raayna's eyes staring back at her, but she couldn't turn around due to the feeling of vomit in her throat. Her hands started to shake violently and her legs started to lose feeling as she thought about what Raayna had just told her.

The bathroom was five feet in front of her, but it felt like China was walking a mile. As soon as she could reach the knob, she opened the restroom door and ran into a stall. Her mostly naked body fell up against the filthy walls, and then she regurgitated into the toilet. Thoughts of Sean walking into the house with a bouquet of roses that she'd tossed on top of him after shooting him to death became unreal as she tried to comprehend what Raayna just told her.

As she heard someone else enter the bathroom, she quickly got up on her two feet, covering her mouth as to not allow her whimpers to be heard. The gunshot repeated itself over and over again in her mind as she watched Sean come into the house holding what she thought were roses and a card to cover up his indiscretions. Her thoughts also went back to the conversation she just had with the woman she found out was having an affair with Sean.

Suddenly the toilet flushed, and the woman who'd followed her into the bathroom walked back out. China once again, fell against the stall walls.

"She's a stripper…" she repeated, shaking her head in disbelief. "He found her exactly where we met," she continued as the tears ran down her eyes like a river. "In the same damn spot!" She banged her fists against the stall, and it was with that bang that she remembered the card that Sean had with the roses. She'd placed it with the other items inside the car. Just then, China bolted from the bathroom to grab her clothes and other items from Jayce's office. While her mind was still on Raayna revealing that they'd broken up, she went ahead and tipped out Jayce while in the office. She knew where to place his money for her night of dancing, and even though he didn't know she was going to leave the club so quickly, she had no choice. She left him extra money just for him doing her the favor along with a note, and she'd never planned on seeing him again. Then, she left the club.

She forced her hair over her face and made eye contact with no one down the graveled walkway. Generally, Jayce had security to walk the dancers out when in the back, but China didn't have time for that. China slammed the door as she got in the driver's seat of her car and pulled out of the lot only to drive down a back road for about a mile before pulling over. She rummaged through her things until she found the greeting card that she angrily snatched from her husband's dying fingers. Then, she took a deep breath and shakily opened the envelope followed with the card.

The greeting card was designed with the hands of a groom and a bride, each of them wearing their wedding rings. Upon first glance, China's breathing became erratic as a result of the fear consuming her as she opened the card. It read:

"China,

You are my life and my love. I don't deserve you at all right now, and these are the reasons why I am writing you, as a confession. The last time you found I was having an affair, I lied when I said it was over. For that, I apologize deeply because as time went on, I wanted it to be over, but I felt I couldn't end it because I'd gotten her pregnant. From that affair, I have another daughter named Synthia. She's nearly the same age as Selah. I've been hiding it from you and Selah because I need you both in my life. I just couldn't keep it from you anymore, and to prove it, I really did end the affair today. I will prove it anytime you want me to...and I will fix this. I promise I will.

We were getting along great for nearly a year. You and I have been happy. That is because it was me... I was the one that needed to change, not you. I couldn't expect you to be happy or me to be happy in this marriage when I was the one always in other women's faces. It took me to really look at myself to know that. I love you. I may even have another daughter, but none of that is enough to make me stay with her and leave you and Selah. If I would have been living right, that pregnancy would have never happened. Please forgive me, China. These roses don't come with guilt this time, baby. They come with a promise and a deep apology. Please, don't leave me. I love you, and I want to continue on only with you."

China's heart nearly burst as the words written inside the card appeared far too real for her to digest after having shot Sean to death inside their home. She began to look around frantically for something to hit or throw because the pain she felt inside was so overwhelming, but when she found nothing to deliver her from her anguish, she began to destroy the greeting card with her bare hands.

"Sean!" she cried out so loudly that if there were passers-by on the road, they would have surely heard her clearly. Her screams were as if she'd lost her only child as she couldn't escape the magnitude of what she'd done to her family. "You never should have lied to me again! I was tired!" She slammed her arms against the steering wheel multiple times and so hard that it was inevitable that she would have bruises the next morning up and down them. She hollered so loudly that she began to feel faint because she was running out of oxygen to breathe. Then, weakly she stated, "Selah, mama is so sorry...God! Jesus! Please, help me! Please, forgive me!" she screamed. The ripped up pieces of the greeting card that were all crumbled in the palms of her hand, she tossed all over the car in a rage at the situation that she'd found herself in. Finally, she began to go into a fit of denial, dismissing the sadness of shooting Sean to death. Instead, she felt like she was justified and his apology came minutes too late. In the end, she convinced herself that she'd always loved him more than he loved her. She then stared at the pieces of greeting card tossed all over her car and stated, "He's a liar. He was gonna do it again. Just like all the other times." She then pulled the weapon she used out from underneath the seat and continued to drive down the road. The rain began to pour, but she drove slowly down the back roads, never turning on her windshield wipers, almost hoping that she would die as well.

Most Wanted Nine

The night ended for Raayna as she finished her set in which she'd pushed back her tears from the breakup with Sean. Earlier in the day when Sean broke up with her, he'd also told her that she would have to go to the courts in order to get child support issued, not because he didn't love taking care of their daughter, but that he didn't want to pay continuously and it not be accounted for later. Other than that, Raayna would be forced to paying her own way with her life from then on out. She was able to do that anyway, but it crushed her that Sean wasn't as in love with her as she thought.

"Hey, girl. You look awful. What's wrong now?" another dancer asked Raayna as she sat down on a stool in the back room. Although the question was loud enough for Raayna to hear, she didn't answer with words. She just shrugged her shoulders and tilted her head to look down at her cell phone.

As she scrolled down the screen of the phone while glancing at a social media site, she ran across something that caught her eye. Raayna immediately sat up from her slouched position on the stool and spun around to place her back to everyone in the room. Quickly, she clicked on the link which took her to the local news website. Her leg bounced up and down as she impatiently waited on the site to load, and when it did, she saw a full headshot of her ex and Synthia's father, Sean.

Raayna plummeted to the floor in heart filled agony, with a wail so loud that every dancer in the room ran her way. They'd danced with Raayna for about two years, but they never knew

132

that Raayna dated a cop. Her personal life was something that was prohibited from being discussed by Sean himself.

With all the attention she'd garnered with her weeping, she quickly looked over her shoulder to see the mountain of women surrounding her. Then, she quickly hit the button of her phone to black out the screen and pushed through the crowd.

"Excuse me, I have to go," she stated as she continued to move between the ladies. One of the women reached for her arm out of concern, but when she did, Raayna pulled back and shoved her out of the way, nearly starting an all out brawl. "I said I have to go! Leave me alone!" Raayna then grabbed whatever items she had with her and ran out of the club…directly into Jayce. When he saw her, he positioned himself in front of her so that she couldn't move.

"What's up, baby girl? The night is still young, and you're leaving already? I have a packed house in there." He leaned in and saw that she was truly distraught, so he pulled her to the side to find out what was wrong. He didn't have to try too hard either because Raayna suddenly spilled all the information as she continued to try and hide her teary eyes from the public.

"Jayce, I have to leave. I can't stay tonight. My baby's father is dead," she cried, dropping herself lower while holding herself up on her knees. "I think I'm going to be sick."

"It's gonna be alright, Raayna. What happened to him? Let me help you to your car."

"He was shot to death, Jayce. He was shot, and…I just saw his wife in here tonight," she confessed to being a mistress.

"His wife? He was married?"

"Yes, but … he loved me, Jayce," she continued, her make-up totally smeared all over her face. "The report says that she is the prime suspect. Can you believe that shit? And her ass was right in here, dancing and got fuckin' paid tonight. I just saw her earlier today with my baby's sister."

"The hell?" Jayce asked looking around confused. "Wait…" he continued, suddenly thinking about China once again. He then backed away from the conversation which could potentially make him a witness to China's whereabouts. "You take your ass on home, get some sleep. I'll check on you. Sorry for your baby's father," he stated, rushing away from Raayna, so much unlike the caring man that she encountered at the door.

Raayna entered her car, unconcerned about Jayce and his getaway, and dialed the police. "Hello? My name is Raayna, and I'm calling because I have information that could help on the shooting of Officer Sean Daniels."

Back inside the strip club, Jayce pushed beyond everyone who was either grabbing at him or calling his name, and when he reached his office, he went inside and locked the door behind him. He checked everywhere in his office for any trace of China being in the club still, but just as he thought, she'd already left. He knew her well enough to know that she would try her best not to bring him into any trouble with her, but now his problem was with Raayna. He spotted the money that China left, and as he grabbed it without even counting it, he pondered a legitimate way to clear the club with no hassle. In the back of his mind, he knew that the cops would be coming any minute, and he knew why – Raayna. The main people he wanted out of the club were those in the VIP section, and he had no other option but to alert them to the cops. He'd happened to have a background into the celebrity's criminal past, and he was going to have to use it as leverage to get him out.

Jayce rose up from the side of the desk, rechecked his office, calmed down as he fixed his suit in front of the mirror, and then headed into the crowd toward the VIP section. The walk seemed to take forever, and everyone knew something was about to happen because Jayce never walked to the VIP section during the entertainment, but he had to at this particular time. The dancers looked up confused, and when Jayce sent them away, the VIPs looked highly irritated as well. Jayce already had the money they'd paid to have a special stripper and the money that China left behind, and he was going to give it all to them for the trouble he was about to put them through.

"Fellas," Jayce greeted all of them, but mainly Bone.

"What's all this cash you got it your hand, man? You comin' for the party, too?" Bone asked as he called more dancers over with his hand, but they hesitated with Jayce's hand going up.

Jayce went and sat next to him, leaned in and whispered in his ear. "You know I don't take anything to do with the business of anyone who comes in my spot, but I just got word that the feds are going to be pushing through here any minute now looking for somebody. Word is that it might be you. I just want to give you the heads up before things go viral, you know how that is with the internet." Jayce had absolutely no idea if Bone was caught up in something illegal currently, but he also knew that when it came down to anyone criminally minded, they didn't want the cops around them anywhere. Jayce didn't even have to name anything specific to create an uneasiness in Bone that caused the rapper to become shifty in his chair.

"The feds, huh? What about?" Bone asked, folding up his money and standing to his feet, causing Jayce to stand with him.

"They didn't say. That's just the word. It could be some kind of questioning or even an arrest warrant. I wish I could tell you, but I don't like heat on my club…"

"Enough said, Jayce. Good looking out. Thanks for the money back and the nice time," he stated as he took the money from Jayce's hand. "Let's go, fellas." Jayce watched as the ladies scattered and the VIP section became empty. The club was still packed, but the main person that China danced for was nowhere to be found, and that was just how Jayce wanted it. With Raayna gone and Bone leaving, there was no one but him for the cops to question that had any idea who China actually was, and he planned on being in denial about her whereabouts at the time.

Jayce walked behind the crew as they left the club, and as he looked outside into the parking lot, he noticed that Raayna was still there. She was on the telephone with someone, and Jayce knew that it was time for him to leave the club as well. Therefore, he let the manager know he was leaving and advised him to call him only if he needed him before closing. Then, he swiftly left. As he got about three minutes down the long winding road, he saw the reflectors from squad cars a short way up. He already knew where they were headed. There was a side road that Jayce decided to turn down, and from there, he dimmed his lights while he turned his car around to face the direction in where the cops were going. As the squad cars passed by, he waited for about one minute before he took the side road back around to the club. As soon as he arrived at the edge of the road where he could clearly see the squad cars, he rolled his window down and spotted Raayna. She was talking to the cops. Therefore, she had to be the one who brought the heat, and it was just as he figured. From there, he drove on home believing that if he was out of sight, he would be out of mind.

Most Wanted Ten

"It doesn't matter. All I'm asking is for a favor, that's all. You can't do that for me, Penelope? After all we've been through, I get nothing from you?" China stated completely soaked in the rain after she cut through yards to reach her sister's house on foot. She'd parked her car behind a store building where there was barely any light, especially in the rain, and from there, walked to Penelope's house with her bag, car keys and a load of cash. "I have money…take care of Selah with it until I send you more." She pulled out the cash and pushed it through the screen door forcefully as Penelope would only allow the screen to open but so much. The cash fell to the floor and scattered at Penelope's feet, but she didn't even look down. Instead, she stared at her sister in disbelief.

"After all *we've* been through?" she repeated, stressing the all inclusiveness of her statement. "Is that what you just said? You mean after all you put *me* through, China, and now your daughter," she said lowering her tone. "And you say it doesn't matter? Don't you know what you've even done, China?" Penelope gazed at her in shock. "Now, get the hell off of my porch," Penelope grumbled fiercely as she shook the screen door of her newly purchased rundown home. "China, move! You can't be here!" she continued to scream at her half-sister in the middle of the night as China relentlessly yanked the screen door against Penelope's wishes.

"You're my sister, Penelope!" China finally gave up and slammed the screen door, resulting in Penelope quickly locking it. "You're supposed to be my blood and you're just gonna leave me out here like this in the rain? You don't know the full story at all!"

"I don't have to know it, dammit, because I saw it!" Penelope yelled as she punched the screen door, her emotions riddled with rage and sadness all at the same time as she looked back into her sister's eyes.

Selah came running from the back room and latched onto Penelope's leg, staring back at China from behind the screen door. "Mama?" She asked half asleep.

"Hey, baby girl. Yeah, it's your mama," China responded out of breath and glaring at her younger sister as she reached at the screen door hoping that her daughter reached back out to her. "Can you put your hand right here, baby? Mama can't come inside because I'm all wet...and I don't want you to catch a cold, you know?"

"I love you, mama. You can come in and dry off, and thank you for letting me stay at Aunt Penelope's house. It's fun over here," said the little girl as she grabbed for the latch of the screen door, but her aunt Penelope moved her hand away.

"Go back to bed. Your mom..."

"I stopped by to see you...before I go back to my new job," China quickly interjected with a lie. "I needed to see that you were okay and if Aunt Penelope is being good to you. Did she feed you, honey?"

"Yes ma'am, and..."

"And go to bed. Your mom," she rolled her eyes so the child wouldn't see her do it, "will be back again. She'll be back soon enough...I'm sure of it."

Selah planted a kiss on the screen door, and it was met with the lips of her mom. That was good enough for her to turn around and go back to bed. China watched beyond her sister as her child turned into the bedroom.

"Leave, China. This time, don't come back. You're on your own." With that, Penelope closed the door, leaving her sister out in the pouring rain.

China stared back at the door's peephole while the rain placed more heaviness on her than what she already carried inside her soul. She slowly turned around as her hair stuck to her face while the rain camouflaged her tears. Suddenly, she snapped out of her saddened daze and realized that she was standing uncovered before neighboring homes to the side and directly in front of her. She could have been seen.

Rushing from the porch, she turned to the back of the house, feeling her way on the side due to the darkness and rain blinding her way, until she felt the crawlspace entrance. As she felt for the latch, it was being held together by a thin, knotted rope, so China kneeled down, unknotted the rope and entered the area beneath the house. She didn't care about any rodents, snakes or anything. The only thing she cared about was being as close to her daughter as possible before having to go on the run again. She'd just become the city's most wanted felon, so she put her head down and cried, with nowhere to go. However, right before sunrise, she was up and ready to run.

China woke up paralyzed with adrenaline as she peeked out of the crawlspace. Each movement felt like a spasm as she tried her best to ease out quietly without disturbing even the grass beneath her fingers as she pushed herself up onto the ground. She knew that when the sun burst through the darkness, there would be enough light for the most elderly person who lived on the block to wake up and start their day. They always peeped out of the window, and she was the last person she wanted them to see.

Leaving her love on the other side of the brick wall, she kissed her hand and touched the bricks of the house because she knew that was as close to Selah as she would get in a long time. When she climbed completely out of the crawlspace, she dusted herself off and immediately started to run. She ran her fastest through the yards and refused to look up for anything because she was in a battle for her freedom. There was no one she could call because the cops would trace her number, and besides that, it was only a matter of time before everyone who was everyone found out that she was the one they were looking for. It was obvious that she was the shooter, especially since Raayna saw her at the club. She'd debated on saying she was kidnapped if ever caught, but as it turned out, her husband's mistress was still a thorn in her side even after their break up and his death. If she spoke to the cops, they would have a strong motive, and there would be nothing to keep her from being hunted. The police force would have no mercy.

"Father God, forgive me," she prayed as she ran as fast as she could. She reached the next street that she had to cross when her car keys fell to the ground. She heard them fall after she'd taken one step off the curb, and when she looked back, she saw the first light come on from inside a home. It stunned her to a standstill for two seconds, but she snapped out of it quickly, retrieved the car keys and turned to run once again. Without paying attention to anything else around her, she stepped out into the street once again, concentrating on making it to the building directly in front of her where her car was parked, when out of the darkness came a patrol cruiser.

China stopped breathing, and the blood that was flowing heavily through her body and pounding on the walls of her blood vessels suddenly felt calm as a result of all her focus going on the squad car. The keys that were held in the air by her finger dangled, moving with the heavy breeze as her eyes locked onto the man in the driver's seat. He stared at her, possibly wondering what she was doing out so early. Therefore, China took a deep breath and tried to calm herself down as she moved her eyes away from the officer's and continued to cross the street, this time, without running. She started to feel her heart beat heavily again as she tried to maintain steady breathing as each step she took on the barren road felt like her ankles were already in shackles.

She'd made it three quarters of the way across the street when from the side of her eye, she saw the red brake lights of the squad car. That was when she sped up, and as soon as her foot hit the edge of the curb, she looked up. The squad car was turning around, and the lights on the top of the car were on and rotating. China began to run.

"No," she repeatedly cried under her breath as she ran behind the building where she parked her car. "No, no, Lord, no… it wasn't supposed to be like this. Please…" she prayed as she fumbled with her keys beside her car, shaking so badly until she couldn't open her door. "Open!" she finally screamed at the top of her lungs. When the door finally opened, she rushed into the car and started it up only to lift her eyes to the windshield and see the officer turning the corner on foot…with his pistol lifted in the air. She hit the gas, barreling directly toward him. The car let out an explosion of power, and as she approached him, he fired one shot. She swerved and then noticed that the officer was someone she knew. It was Officer Camden…Sean's old partner. He pointed the gun directly in her face as she drove by but didn't pull the trigger. Instead, he called her name, and all China heard as she drove by was her name in the wind.

For moments, all China heard was her own breathing as the road ahead of her narrowed before her very eyes, and as she took a quick check into the rearview mirror, she saw the squad car being driven by Officer Camden coming behind her. China floored it as she turned her head back in the direction of Penelope's house to imagine seeing her daughter for what could be her last time as a free woman.

"Baby, mama's not gonna get caught. Selah, I will always be here for you," she spoke to Selah which gave her the willpower to not give up. She glared at Officer Camden through the mirror and reached for her pistol, her thought process being that if Officer Camden already let her drive off without killing her the first time, then she had his favor if only for a little while.

Officer Camden used to be close with her and Sean. He was even present for the birth of Selah. It was only shortly after Sean's promotion that they had to spit up. China never knew that on this day it would be Officer Camden to chase her on the ride for her life.

The interstate was only a minute down the road, and China knew if she could get there, she would be free for as long as she needed to be. From there, she would lose Officer Camden and then ditch her car to go on the run. She had six hundred dollars on her person after leaving the rest to Penelope. On top of that, she had several people that could hide her out until she left the state. The only problem was losing Officer Camden before he called for back-up, and the way it seemed, he was stalling because of his love for her and her family.

China slowed the car all the way down to allow Officer Camden to catch up to her, even nearly pull up beside her. From there, China took the chance of rolling her window down as she watched the officer carefully. From the side of her eye, she saw herself closing the distance quickly between herself and the off ramp, and finally, she heard Officer Camden call her name.

"China, pull over. Back up is on the way, now pull over!" he shouted, but China only stared back into his eyes and yelled back.

"I didn't do anything!"

The off ramp was directly in front of her car, and as she pretended to pull over right before passing the off ramp, she quickly darted onto it. Nearly losing control of the car as a result of how much speed she put on the gas, she skidded onto the ramp and bolted onto the interstate. China's heart felt like it could burst from her chest as she turned the rear view mirror to watch as Officer Camden swerved his car back around to enter the interstate behind her.

"Dammit, go!" she screamed at her sports car. She'd gained enough distance between them that she floored it on the partially empty road. She passed drivers on the wet road as she concentrated on losing him at the next exit which would set her on a long winding road and then back on the interstate in the opposite direction. From the other side of the road, she spotted another police car who spotted her as well, and immediately put on his lights and went in pursuit by cutting across the median. Now she wasn't just on the run from a friend, she was on the run from cops with absolutely no mercy. On top of that, her way out had just disappeared as the second cop closed in.

China stared at her cell phone and decided to use it for the first time. She voice dialed Penelope, but when the phone rang, she got no answer. Then, she quickly hung up and called Jayce, however, after letting the phone ring only once, she hung up and twisted the wheel of the car so hard that it barreled onto the next exit, nearly running over into the dense bushes and trees at the edge of the road. With both hands she threw the car back into the road, and the car went into a full spin, leaving China out of control of the car. She screamed in horror until the car came to an abrupt stop, then she punched the accelerator, only to find that while her car raced down the street, a helicopter came flying over head.

"Leave me alone!" she screamed, at a loss for what to do next because in reality, there was nothing to do next but drive until she couldn't drive anymore. The interstate was a long one, and more people would be up getting ready for work at any minute. Because she was gripping the steering wheel so tightly and concentrating on not getting into a wreck, she forgot to look back at what was behind her. The small amount of cars that were hastily driving to their whereabouts suddenly began to pullover and come to complete stops on the side of the road. When China took another glance back behind her, the sirens blared back at her as there were not only two police cars on her trail, but several. That was when her cell phone rang. It was an unidentifiable number, so she knew it was them.

Most Wanted Eleven

Penelope woke up to a stirring Selah in the hallway. She'd already let her new job know the situation of her brother-in-law's death, therefore, she wasn't going to go in to work in order to get things situated with the family. It was only reaching seven o'clock in the morning, and Penelope had been up for most of the night, trying to read her Bible and pray mostly, for strength and wisdom on what to do with her life now that Selah was in it for seemed to be the long haul. She also prayed for her sister, China, despite their arguments and shouting matches because she still loved her, but all her life she felt that China brought her extra stress that she didn't want. This situation was the worst with the shooting of Sean. Penelope didn't know exactly how to feel, but she hoped that through her tears that she cried all night long that God would decipher them all so that nothing would destroy her or Selah in the end. She'd battled depression before, and didn't want to suffer through it anymore.

Penelope called out of her room for Selah as she laid on the bed, attempting to remain shielded from her young niece as much as possible as a result of her breaking down and crying sporadically since the incident. "Selah, baby, are you okay? I'm just lying down in here. I'll be up cooking something for you in a while. Are you hungry? You can watch television, baby."

"Morning, Aunt Penelope. I'm just playing with my bouncy ball you got for me. Not hungry yet, but I can watch T.V. for real? Mama, never lets me watch T.V. this early."

"Well, it's Saturday, so the cartoons are on just about every channel it seems. Do you know how to change the…"

"Yes, ma'am, I sure do! I'll find them!"

"Okay, sweetheart," she choked out, holding back her tears imagining what was going to happen with Selah as she glanced over at the pile of money China left with her. She'd already placed it in three envelopes for Selah because she couldn't afford to care for her without the monetary help. China would have never brought her the money unless she knew she wasn't going to return soon. From the looks of everything, Penelope knew it was going to be a very long time before her sister would see the light of day…freely. It was that and her visual of Sean lying dead that would plague her for life.

Instead of remaining in the bed, she realized she did have to get up soon and place her emotions to the side to take care of Selah. Therefore, she walked up to the front door and made certain that the door was locked, and then walked back into her bedroom with the key. She would normally allow the key to remain inside the door's bolt lock, however, with Selah in the house, she didn't want her to open the door for anyone or leave without her knowledge.

Penelope then hopped into the shower, allowing the water to flow down her face as she finally let out the cry that she needed to release. "Lord, please, forgive her. Please, forgive me. I don't know what to do except live one day at a time. I need you, Jesus, please," she continued to cry as she listened out for Selah. She heard the television playing, and before she turned off the water, she thought she also heard the telephone ringing. Therefore, she shut down the shower and listened again, but she no longer heard the ringing of the house phone. Slowly, and more relaxed, she started to dry off with a bright blue and fluffy towel. Her eyes were puffy when she looked at her reflection in the mirror, and anyone who was wise enough could tell she'd been troubled throughout the night. Without anymore regard for her appearance, she wrapped her hair in a bun and then heard Selah's voice. It sounded like she was talking to someone. Quickly, Penelope wrapped the towel around her body and left the bathroom.

Most Wanted Twelve

China continued to watch the phone ring, but she never picked up. As soon as it stopped ringing, however, she snatched the phone and slowed the car down in order to control the situation better than what she had. By that time, squad cars were everywhere, and there was a countless number behind her and in front of her, supposedly clearing the road of innocent citizens.

China's eyes were filled with tears as she called Penelope's home. As the telephone rang, she looked up in the sky and saw the helicopter continuing to keep an eye on her as she continued down the interstate. Someone picked up the phone.

"Hello? Selah," China recognized her daughter's voice immediately, although she wasn't expecting it. "I love you so much, baby," she sniffled.

"Mama, what's wrong?"

"Nothing, baby. What are you doing up so early? Shouldn't you be in the bed?"

"Aunt Penelope said I can watch cartoons, but she's in the bathroom now though. She's even letting me control the remote! See, watch." Selah begins to flip through the stations slowly, and then she stops. "Mom, mommy, look! You're on the T.V."

"What, baby?" China questioned her in a startled tone. "Mommy's not on television."

"Yes you are. It's a picture of you next to... Mama, they even have your car on there, too! I see you driving...with daddy and all his cars," she continued excited. "Come get me, Ma! It's a parade. Aunt Penelope! Come here!" she called as she jumped up and down on the sofa.

"Selah," China started to cry as she noticed a line of police cars up ahead blocking her getaway. "Selah, baby, you're right. Mama is in a parade, but I need you to turn the television off now. You know my rules about the T.V."

"Mama, come get me. I can see you. I'm gonna give you a kiss, too. Here." Selah ran over to the television and smooched her lips up against it. "There, Mama, see."

"I see, baby," China began to cry as her car came to a stop, completely blocked by police cars all around. "I'm kissing you back. I left you with a lot of money, okay, and that is to take care of you for now. Mommy also has some friends who will bring you some more anytime I call for them, okay? Do you know something, baby?"

"You love me?"

"You got it. I love you more than life itself. Now, I need you to please, baby, turn off the television. Mommy, has to get out of the car soon, okay?"

"Ma, where's dad?"

"Listen, Selah!" China shouted into the telephone as she watched the cops aiming their pistols at her on every side.

"Mama, why are they holding guns at you?" she started to cry. "Tell daddy to stop it! Aunt Penelope! Help my mama!" she dropped the telephone and ran down the hall, only to run directly into her in the hallway.

"For those just tuning in, it was yesterday evening when Officer Sean Daniels was shot and killed in his home, apparently right at his front door. His wife, China Daniels, is the prime suspect for the shooting," the newscaster spoke, and her words hit Penelope like a ton of bricks to the chest. The newscaster continued, "And as of yet, we have no details of what led to such a brutal shooting, however, as of right now, police have just ended a high speed chase in the middle of the interstate with the suspect, China Daniels, behind the wheel. She is believed to..."

Penelope fell to her knees as Selah continued to yank her by her wrist. As she crawled behind a screaming and crying Selah, who by that time had already run back to the television, pointing at her mom exiting the car, Penelope got a full scope of her sister surrounded. She also spotted China holding her cell phone up to her ear. Immediately, Penelope ran to her house phone that she spotted off the hook.

"Hello, China!" she cried. "Oh Jesus, China, put the gun down."

"I love you, Penelope. Take care of my baby girl, okay. You got to turn off that television. I'm sorry for everything, but if they shoot at me, Penelope, I'm shooting back so turn off that T.V. and put Selah back on the phone."

"Please, China, don't do this. Dear God, I beg you... Selah!" she called frantically at her niece until she had to yank her from the television screen. The remote control was nowhere in clear sight, and Penelope wasn't about to put the phone down. She grabbed Selah by the chest and threw her against hers, facing away from the television, both of their bodies slammed up against the bottom of the sofa.

"Put my baby on the phone, Penelope. Tell her that her daddy isn't doing this. Tell her he was trying to save my life, and that's how he died. I fuckin' swear if they shoot me...I'm his wife. He was cheating on me again, Penelope, and he just didn't stop until…" she wept, staring at all the officers until she spotted Officer Camden approaching her cautiously.

"China, you're out of your mind! Put the gun down!"

"Mommy!" Selah screamed, fighting to see the television.

Penelope watched as China walked forward, and then she shut her eyes, fearful of what would happen next on the television. Her eyes jolted open when she heard the phone hang up.

Most Wanted Thirteen

"China, please, put the gun down. You have to listen to me, China. Look, I'm not even pointing my gun at you either, and even though you aren't pointing it at me, you have to drop it to the ground."

"I'm going away for life, Camden, and you know it, don't you? So what's the difference right now? You should have just let me go," she cried. "And now my baby girl is watching…"

"What do you mean, China? Come on, put the gun down. Is Selah in the car?" he asked, waving the cops to not shoot as he moved closer. He then peeped over into the sports car but couldn't get a visual of anyone else inside the car. "China, if there's a child in the car…"

"She's not in the car, Camden," she laughed in slight hysterics over all she'd done. "She's watching on T.V." Then, she tilted her head and questioned him oddly, "You really called the helicopter on me, and got me all splattered on the news? Are you gonna shoot me in front of her, Camden?" she stated lifting her arms up to the side with the gun still in her hand.

"China, put the damn gun down now!" he finally shouted, drawing his weapon. "Listen, China, they will kill you!"

"Did you know, Camden? Did you know that Sean was cheating on me and had a daughter with his mistress?"

"China, come on…"

"Answer me!"

"China, yes, yes...but he told me he was going to break it off. I know for a fact he loved you. Even though we weren't partners anymore, we still talked. You know that, China."

"Camden, I messed up," she stammered, moving her hand to wipe her face of the tears, but none of the officers shot. "He came in after I saw him with her yesterday, and they were together...but then I shot him. It was easy, Camden. He used to hit me before all this...I just never told you. He tell you that?"

"China, stop moving your arms and get on the ground!"

"Why?" China asked him before turning her head to look at the other officers and then up at the helicopter. "Close your eyes, baby!" she shouted referring to Selah. The tears floated away as her hair blew in the wind. There she stood all alone with no desire to spend the rest of her life in prison, so she made her final decision. "Selah, I love you!" Then, she lifted the gun at the officer and fired off one shot, purposely tilting it in the air, and that was the end.

Penelope dropped Selah underneath her to the floor, struggling to keep her down as she screamed louder than she'd ever screamed before, even fought harder than she'd ever fought before, as she ended up catching a glimpse of her mother falling to the street. Penelope struggled to breathe as she watched her sister become riddled with bullets and fall to the ground. Her hands gripped Selah as much as she could while covering her eyes.

Atop Selah, Penelope sobbed as her niece finally gave up her physical struggle and settled on weeping until she fell asleep. Penelope just sat there on the floor for hours, watching repeats of what happened to her sister with the phone still off the hook and Selah asleep in her arms.

"It was only yesterday that somehow the family of a well known and loved police officer, Sean Daniels, was torn apart when his own wife pointed a pistol at him as he walked through the door of his home and shot him to death. What you see now on the screen is the tragic ending of the high speed chase that started early this morning, with his wife, China Daniels, being gunned down after she opened fire on police officers. The scene was very graphic…she raises her gun as we see here and fires on the officer, barely missing him. As you can see, the officers surrounding her fired as well as the one standing directly in front of her. It's amazing that she missed him, almost as if she did it on purpose. You can actually hear the seconds go by before the other officers shot her. It's all just so tragic, and word has come in that her own child possibly saw her mother get shot down on the television. There will be more from this report later…" the television newscaster continued, and finally, Penelope turned for the first time from her traumatic gaze at the television, reached slowly for the telephone, and hung it up. She then got up with Selah and went to bed. It was only twenty minutes later that there was a knock at the door. Penelope sat up from the bed, but didn't move anymore.

Most Wanted Fourteen

Jayce backed away from his television screen, holding in his tears. He'd driven all the way back to his home after watching Raayna reveal all that she thought China could have done to the police. Regardless of how he felt about any other girl at the club, he felt the most about China. He'd once been in love with her, and his feelings for her never fully subsided. He'd just finished watching her be shot to death on television, and forgetting about it was the last thing he would do.

There was something that Jayce always said he would do, and he remembered China screaming it at him when she was at the club just hours before her death. She screamed to him *"You owe me!"* As China's voice rang over and over in his head, he dug into his pocket and opened the note she left in with the money. The note told him where her daughter was located and how to get there, along with a phone number. He'd made up his mind. He would go to the house, and that was what he did.

When he arrived at the house, it was early, only a couple of hours since the shooting aired live on television. There was no answer at the door, and he knocked on the door even harder. After about four minutes, someone opened the door.

Penelope stood there at her front door expressionless while staring at a man she'd only spoken to a couple of times in her life due to her affiliation with China. She had no idea what he was doing at her home, nor did she know how he found out where she lived. Although those questions were floating in her mind, she didn't have the energy to ask, so she just looked at him oddly.

155

"Penelope, I know what has happened, and I'm sorry," he started. "I came to be certain that you and Selah, China's daughter, are okay before I head out of town."

It was already his plan to leave town until all of the questioning by authorities died down. He wasn't sure what kind of questioning they would have since China had already been shot, but to be in front of the cops wasn't his pleasure because his own hands weren't squeaky clean. It even made him nervous just standing at Penelope's front door as he questionably looked at Penelope who wasn't moving a muscle after he spoke. He realized something was seriously wrong, rooting from the obvious.

"Penelope, can I come on in?" When she didn't answer, Jayce grabbed the handle of the screen door. "Let me in, Penelope. I can already see that…"

All of a sudden, she began to weep. Tears flowed as she continued to stand there as if she'd lost her mind, not saying one word to Jayce. He then looked around, feeling a bit uneasy, but continued to open the screen door slowly, and before he even stepped foot inside the house, Penelope collapsed. He leaned inside the door quickly to grab her before she hit the floor, causing him to fall to his knees with her in his arms. Jayce then moved her over and shut the door behind them. As he leaned his back up against the door, he pulled Penelope into his arms and allowed her to cry. Her moans were as if she'd lost her own child, and Jayce felt helpless as she held on to his arm tightly, squeezing it like a person that could literally do nothing else to ease the agony.

"Penelope," he whispered her name, but she failed to respond. It was only minutes later that he heard shuffling in the back room, so he stood himself up while helping a distraught Penelope off of the floor and to the sofa. Then, he walked to the back room, leaving Penelope rocking back and forth on the chair. As he walked to the back room, he didn't know what to expect. He'd remembered running into China with her daughter only when she was an infant, but aside from that short time, he didn't know much else about the child. The only thing he knew was that he wanted to do right by China because she no longer had parents of her own. Even though he wasn't the best role model, he would be before her eyes because he knew that China would want that.

When he looked into the bedroom, he saw a little girl. She wasn't crying. She was only sitting on the bed with her head down to the floor.

"Are you China's daughter?" he spoke.

"Yes sir. Is my mom here yet? I want to go home now. I want her off the T.V."

Jayce realized immediately that the young girl had already seen her mother being shot. Not understanding how he should deal with the situation, and also not wanting to be caught at the house when and if the police came by because he already knew that Penelope was her last living relative in the city, he reached for five hundred dollars and showed it to her.

"Come here. Isn't your name Selah, sweetheart?" he asked as she got off the bed and walked toward him.

"Where is my Aunt Penelope? What's your name?"

"My name is Jay," he said, purposely dropping the latter part of his name off. "I got some money for you, just in case you need it. I am going to give it to your aunt. She's sitting out there…feeling bad in the stomach, so I need you to…"

"I'm hungry, Jay."

"Alright look, let me go look in the kitchen, and see what I can find you while I talk to your aunt. We will make something for you together. In the meantime, you stay put. Is that alright?"

"Yes sir." Selah climbed back into the bed and shut her eyes to Jayce's relief, and then he rushed back out to Penelope who was still rocking. As he turned the corner into the living room, Penelope turned her head to look back at him, finally saying something without being probed to do so.

"She always managed to make our lives hell…me and Mama. I know you still love her, Jayce, but there is a side to her that you obviously never knew. She would always have a way," she stated with her face as expressionless as someone who is fast asleep, "Of taking the happiness away from us."

"All siblings go through different things, Penelope. We all have disagreements…" he said trying to make things better, but Penelope shot him a terrible glance that made him stop talking.

"Disagreements? She left her daughter here once, for no reason, and if she had a reason, she definitely didn't tell me. I had to watch after her with Sean…her husband…until she decided in herself that she was finished doing whatever she had to do. Then she returned, and everything was supposed to be forgotten? Oh and how perfect her life was, you know, while we all carried the weight…all the time. With all the worry she put us through, and me and mom ended up poorer than her." She stared at the black television. "And now look…she's gone and shot her husband…Selah's father." She cut her eyes back to him. "What did he ever do to her but take good care of her? I never heard one bad thing about him, but I'm sure she, if she was here, could tell me why she shot him, huh? She probably had

this shit planned all along! Claimed he was cheating. Really?"
Penelope screamed. "She was fuckin' crazy then, and she's…"

"Wait, Penelope," he interjected, a bit frustrated at the
sound of Penelope making derogatory statements about her
deceased sister. "I don't know everything about China, but one
thing I do know is that she loved you. I don't know about what
she planned either, but what I do know is that she was going
through things you knew nothing about. Her husband wasn't a
saint, P. He really did have another family, a whole other
daughter and everything." He placed the money in her hand, as
she stared at him confused. "Now, that may not be a reason to
kill someone or abandon your daughter, but I can tell you that
she obviously had no one to talk or turn to that wouldn't fuck up
her mind even worse. She loved your ass enough to send you
and your mom money when she was stripping, didn't she? You
needed the money didn't you? I know about that because I was
with her. I'm gonna take care of you and Selah, too, because you
two were her life. You got shit fucked up…worrying about
yourself. She was obviously putting on a front for everyone,
especially you. She's dead," he then stated, causing more tears
to run down Penelope's face. Finally, he softened his tone
realizing that he may have said too much. "Life has to go on
though. You got baby girl back there, and I'm here for as long as
I can be." He looked at the money. "There's more where that
came from, and you'll get it." At that he headed toward the door.

"Wait…what other family?" she called behind him,
finally able to hear something beyond her bitterness and loss.
"Sean was seeing other people, and she didn't tell me? Selah has
siblings?" Penelope felt lost, and suddenly, she felt like she
never even knew China. It was like she was a total stranger.

He turned back around. "All I know is that, yeah, Selah
has a sister. She's her age matter of fact because I just found out
that I know the girl he was messing with. Hell, that's probably

why she fucked him up with that gun if you ask me. I just found out about Raayna."

"Raayna…is that her name?" Penelope cut him off. "The mistress?"

"Yeah…"

"Where does she live? Do you know? I mean, Selah, now that she has no one else but me, needs to know her sister, don't you think so?" Penelope asked, rising from her seat and moving toward Jayce who noticed her change in demeanor. "This will at least give me some hope for Selah in the future. Who knows what will happen to me," she continued, batting her eyes at the window instead of staring Jayce in the face.

Jayce didn't think twice about what she said, but looked at her peculiarly. He'd never known of Penelope to be a dangerous type girl. As for as he was concerned, she was level-headed and extremely responsible, according to the way China would laud her. He remembered the good stories that China would tell him about her sister, so he wasn't exactly happy about the bad way that Penelope was trying to portray her. Putting that aside because he knew that she may just be going through the range of emotions, he revealed the location where he may find her.

"You can find her over there in Dew Crossing. I can't tell you the address, but if you really think that would be best for Selah, she drives a white Audi with pink tags and pink seat covers. Can't miss that. If you see it, then that's her. Your sister was a lot of things, but one thing she wasn't was a backstabber. She did what she had to do, tried to protect everyone. It was in her own way, which wasn't always the best way, but she loved you. I can say that. I'll be looking out for you and Selah the best way I can until things get better."

"Thank you…and I love my sister, Jayce. My disagreements with her never made me stop loving her once."

Jayce just nodded and left. As soon as he got into his car and drove down the road, he passed by a squad car. From his rear view mirror, he watched as it stopped directly in front of Penelope's house.

Most Wanted Fifteen

"You are her closest and only surviving relative, and we truly apologize for having to tell you..."

"I watched it you know. Her daughter and I, we watched it. How you gunned her down."

"She aimed..."

"I saw it," Penelope interrupted again, batting a tear from her eye, refusing to appear victimized before the officers whom she saw as the murderers of her sister. Emotionally, Penelope was torn between what was right and what was wrong, and that began to wear on her psychological state. "I saw what she did, and I also saw what you did."

"Well, ma'am, we hate that we had to do that because we know Officer & Mrs. Daniels. We loved them both, however, Mrs. Daniels confessed to the homicide. If you would like to hear what happened, we will tell you what we believe drove your sister to killing your brother in law, our fellow officer."

Penelope sat there for a moment, and then she stood up to go and close the hall door in order to block the conversation from Selah's ears. When she sat back down, she was prepared to listen, no matter how difficult it was.

"We found ripped up pieces of paper in her car after your sister's death, and as the evidence goes and from what she told Officer Camden before she was shot, he was involved with another woman. His affair lasted for quite some time because he has a..."

I Will Do Anything For Her

"Daughter. Another daughter."

"Yes, so you knew?"

"No."

There was an awkward silence as the officers expected her to say more than the answer that she'd given them. However, although far more innocent than her sister, she wasn't exactly street insensitive either. She knew that what people don't say for themselves to the cops, they generally don't want others saying to them either. Besides that, Penelope had no more lives to save but Selah's.

"When your brother in law walked inside the home, he was shot immediately. There was evidence, based on several witnesses in the neighborhood, that they'd seen your sister enter the home prior to Officer Daniels. They say when Officer Daniels got home, he had roses in his hand presumably for his wife. We found the roses inside her car. She was indeed the shooter, and the roses backed up her confession. She wouldn't put the gun down, Mrs. Greenwater, so we had to..."

"Kill her." Penelope's stare penetrated the officers who could only stare back at her sorrowfully and apologize for the life they had to take because, in their words, they had no other option. The words *no other option* began to fester in Penelope's heart and mind. Even after the officer's left her home, she felt like those words gave her life a whole new meaning.

A couple of days went by as she started Selah in a brand new affordable daycare closer to where she lived while Penelope prepared to go back to work. Although Penelope had a funeral to plan, there were many hours in the day to spend staring at the walls all alone. She felt she needed that time because she had no other family at all, not even a church family because she'd long stopped going after having resorted to just reading her Bible and not fellowshipping with other church members. It wasn't because she didn't want to fellowship, but it was because she needed to earn a living. Working took up her time. Even her way of earning a living had been snatched from her since Selah became her responsibility, leaving her to accept handouts, something she never wanted to do.

Her happiness was quickly deteriorating into a depression as she felt that her own life was being held up by a loaded gun that continued to shoot, missing her while destroying everything around her. The walls then began to tell her that she had no other option.

As she slid down on the bathroom floor, she began to cry for her sister as she remembered the nightmares that she'd had each night since that morning she saw China shot to death. With the piece of paper that she held inside her left hand, she began to write on it with an ink pen. Blood started to drip on the paper as a result of her catching a nose bleed. Stress would generally cause that to happen all of her life, but her stress level would increase when she located the mistress named Raayna. She found that location after dropping Selah off at a new daycare.

Penelope found herself at the library scanning through the neighborhood that Jayce told her about. She'd hardly ever used satellite imagery provided by search engines, however, she felt it was high time she found out who the loaded gun was aiming at her sister's family for so long, causing her sister to retaliate in all the wrong ways, thus, getting her shot to death. She scanned each street of the small neighborhood for the car Jayce described to her - white with pink details inside and out. She clicked the arrow up and down the streets, and after about thirty minutes, she'd run into something that she'd hoped for. The satellite imagery had a photo of the car she was in search of, and it was parked in front of a place of residence. She then left the library towards her home where she'd end up unlocking her small safe.

As Penelope stood up from the bathroom floor from feeling faint, she walked back toward the bathroom sink to clean her nose, leaving the pen and note on the bathroom floor. She continued to remember how she'd had China all wrong when all China was ever doing was destroying her life to make it better for the people she loved, the only way she knew how at the time. It was wrong but it was her way. Penelope started to cry again, and then, she picked up the gun that was on the bathroom counter that she'd retrieved from her safe. From there, she walked out her front door.

She headed over to the neighborhood and found the mistress' home. The car was in the driveway just as it was on the internet map. From there, Penelope pulled up right beside it, stepped out of the car without turning her car off, and walked to the front door.

The day was a pleasant one, and the birds were chirping from the tree tops. Peaceful noise surrounded her as she adored the pink sign created by a child that hung from the front door that stated in big letters and misspelled – NOK REAL LOUD. Glitter was splashed onto glue all over the paper, and Penelope did exactly what the sign told her to do. In seconds, the door was opened, and a young girl stood in front of her who looked just like her deceased brother in law, Sean, but not her sister.

"How many times have I told you not open this door, Synthia, huh? Move," a woman exclaimed while moving the young child from the door, feeling less threatened when she saw that there was a lady standing three feet back from the entrance with her hands behind her back. "May I help you?" Raayna asked.

Penelope spoke quickly. "Hi, and yes. I'm a member of the family...Sean's family." It pained her to not say China's sister, but she knew that would possibly hinder why she was there in the first place. "I am told that he has a daughter that could possibly be my relative."

A tear fell from Raayna's eye, and then she glanced down at Synthia who held on to her leg. "Yes, please, come on inside." She opened the door wider and allowed Penelope entry. Then, she looked down at Synthia again. "This is Synthia... and you are?"

Penelope looked down at Synthia who stuck her head out from around her mom's leg and then took off up the staircase in giggles. "She looks just like Sean," Penelope continued as she watched Raayna close the door. When Raayna turned back around to face her, Penelope held a gun to her head. Although Raayna's screams were deafening, they didn't silence the words of the officer who told her about how her sister died, like they had no other option. The more she screamed, the more Penelope recalled her sister falling behind the calculated misdeeds of Raayna with her brother in law, and she finally felt like she needed to protect her sister for once in her life.

"I'm China's sister." Penelope, then, pulled the trigger and shot Raayna directly in the center of her head. As Raayna's body fell, her screaming stopped, but more began. Penelope glanced to her left side and saw little Synthia crying her eyes out while staring at her mother who lay dead in front of the door.

Penelope leaned down calmly to her and spoke, having already lost her mind. "Let's go get your sister, baby. She's about to be all you got in this world." From there, she lifted Synthia while covering her mouth and carried her to the car as she kicked and screamed. It wasn't long before Penelope picked up Selah from daycare and they all headed off, driving into nowhere, with all the money Penelope had hidden in her home along with the extra funds from Jayce.

She would drive until there was nowhere left to drive, live where no one wanted to ever live, and eat how they wanted to eat all the while training the sisters to never turn their backs on each other...for anyone.

When the cops entered the home of Penelope, they found the blood stained note left in the bathroom that read – *I had no other option.* Penelope had just become one of America's most wanted felons.

THE END